CINNAMON CIDER WHISKEY

IT'S ALL IN THE WHISKEY

JEN TALTY

JUPITER PRESS

PRAISE FOR JEN TALTY

"*Deadly Secrets* is the best of romance and suspense in one hot read!" *NYT Bestselling Author Jennifer Probst*

"A charming setting and a steamy couple heat up the pages in a suspenseful story I couldn't put down!" *NY Times and USA today Bestselling Author Donna Grant*

"Jen Talty's books will grab your attention and pull you into a world of relatable characters, strong personalities, humor, and believable storylines. You'll laugh, you'll cry, and you'll rush to get the next book she releases!" Natalie Ann USA Today Bestselling Author

"I positively loved *In Two Weeks*, and highly recommend it. The writing is wonderful, the story is fantastic, and the characters will keep you coming back for more. I can't wait to get my hands on future installments of the NYS Troopers series." *Long and Short Reviews*

"*In Two Weeks* hooks the reader from page one. This is a fast paced story where the development of the romance grabs you emotionally and the suspense keeps you sitting on the edge of your chair. Great characters, great writing, and a believable plot that can be a warning to all of us." *Desiree Holt, USA Today Bestseller*

"*Dark Water* delivers an engaging portrait of wounded hearts as the memorable characters take you on a healing journey of love. A mysterious death brings danger and intrigue into the drama, while sultry passions brew into a believable plot that melts the reader's heart. Jen Talty pens an entertaining romance that grips the heart as the colorful and dangerous story unfolds into a chilling ending." *Night Owl Reviews*

"This is not the typical love story, nor is it the typical mystery. The characters are well rounded and interesting." *You Gotta Read Reviews*

"Murder in Paradise Bay is a fast-paced romantic thriller with plenty of twists and turns to keep you guessing until the end. You won't want to miss this one..." *USA Today bestselling author Janice Maynard*

BOOK DESCRIPTION

Will they find the strength to overcome the shadows of their pasts and forge a future together, or will the haunting secrets of Whiskey Ranch consume them both?

Cinnamon Cider Whiskey is desperate to escape the clutches of her abusive husband. Seeking solace and safety, she returns to Whiskey Ranch, where her heart first found its rhythm. But her husband, consumed by possessiveness and a twisted sense of control, refuses to let her go.

The ghosts of a failed relationship haunt Austin Sawyer, his heart still mending from the shattered pieces. Just as he begins to rebuild his life, his ex-girlfriend mysteriously disappears, leaving a trail of unanswered questions.

As fate intertwines their lives again, Cinnamon and Austin are drawn together by a shared past and desire for justice. With danger lurking in the shadows, they must navigate treacherous waters, unraveling a web of secrets and deceit. In a race against time, Cinnamon and Austin must confront their own demons and fight for their lives, all while discovering that their love, though tested and scarred, may be the key to unlocking the dark secrets that threaten to tear their world apart.

For my readers…you rock!

PROLOGUE

ONE YEAR AGO...

Austin Sawyer took off his cowboy hat and raked a hand across the top of his head. He sucked in a deep breath, holding it for a count of five. A dozen cuss words filled his brain and he desperately wanted to let them roll off his tongue. However, he'd been working on his anger issues and there was no point in using foul language to get his point across. "I'm not moving and that's final."

"You promised this was a trial. That we'd see if we liked it. Well, I hate it here and I'm not staying." Charity stomped her high heel into the dirt and twisted her ankle.

He reached out, curling his fingers around her forearm. The last thing he wanted was to spend an afternoon in the emergency room listening to

Charity berate nice nurses and doctors for doing their job while she behaved like an entitled brat.

"Let go of me." She jerked free, stumbling backward into the fence. She steadied herself, brushing the hair from her face.

"I've told you a million times you're going to break your neck wearing those things out here." He shook his head. "You should wear the nice boots I bought you. They have a small heel and—"

"No way. Not happening. And I'm not staying in this hellhole a second longer." She planted her hands on her hips. "There is absolutely nothing for me to do here."

He sighed. It was time to be honest. He'd avoided this conversation for a couple of weeks and it wasn't fair to either of them for him to continue doing it. The worst part was she hadn't seemed to care that he'd been sleeping in the guest room. Or at least she hadn't questioned the fact he'd been coming home late. When he'd mentioned it, she shrugged and said she understood or was glad he hadn't woken her because he stank like horse shit anyway. "You're right. You don't fit in at the ranch."

"Finally, we see eye to eye. Now, when can we leave?"

"*We* don't." He adjusted his Stetson and leaned

against the fence. "I think it's best if you pack up your things and move back to Boise, alone. You and I are oil and water. Tom is a much better match."

Her mouth dropped open and her eyes went wide. It wasn't often that Charity could be rendered speechless and Austin had to rein in a smile. He shouldn't enjoy this moment. However, a lightness filled his mind and soul. Coming back to Whiskey Ranch after being gone so long had been exactly what he needed, only he brought extra baggage that he should have left in Boise.

There had been so many signs that he chose to ignore. He'd wanted to put the pains of the past behind him and he thought he had. However, being back at the ranch had proven that while he could live his life, he had no room for romance in his heart.

She cleared her throat. "I don't know what you're talking about."

"Come on. Let's be realistic and honest." He tipped his hat back and lowered his chin. "You've been cheating on me for months with Tom. I honestly don't know why you agreed to move out here with me when you'd rather be with him." He pointed to the ring on her finger. "I do want that back. It was my mother's."

She narrowed her stare and pursed her lips. Something she did while contemplating her next words.

This should be interesting. Charity could be as sweet as a peach. She had a soft side that not many people got to see, but he had. He did care for her more than any other woman he'd dated in the last fifteen years. However, when she didn't get her way, she would stop at nothing to make it happen, and that was something he could no longer live with.

"You don't know what it's been like for me. We had a nice life in Boise, and then out of the blue you started talking about how you wanted to move back to Buhl and to this ranch." She tilted her head. "I couldn't help but wonder if maybe that Cinnamon girl had moved back or something. I know you still have feelings for her and don't deny that fact." She glared, casting daggers in his direction. "You're the one calling for honesty here."

"Cinnamon is married and lives in Idaho Falls." If Charity hadn't been cheating on him, he could understand why Charity would bring up Cinnamon. He'd been madly in love with her since he'd been a freshman in high school and she in seventh grade. He'd known her his entire life, but poor choices on both their parts had put an end to that relationship. "She's not the reason I wanted to come back. As a matter of fact, and you know this, if she'd been here, I wouldn't have entertained the job opportunity when JW offered it to me." It was a lie, but Austin didn't owe Charity an explanation. She'd been the one who destroyed any chance they had at a future. Not him and his sudden need to learn more about what had really happened to Cinnamon. "But let's be clear about the truth. You've been cheating on me for at least six months before we moved here and I'm the fool who let it go on." He took her left hand and wiggled the ring off her finger. He slipped it into his pocket.

She gasped. "You don't know what you're talking about."

"I read the texts on your phone."

"You had no right to go through my cell without my permission."

He laughed. "That's just it. You asked me to look something up and a message from him popped up on the screen. I have to say, I was a little shocked at the dirty talk. That's not like you." She always acted so prim and proper. At first, he thought it was sweet. Something different, but it had grated on his nerves in the last year. If he even said anything remotely sexual, she got all weird.

She lifted her hand as if to slap him, but dropped it to her side just as quickly. "I'll be gone by morning. I'd appreciate it if you stayed somewhere else tonight."

"Fair enough." This had gone better than he'd expected. Part of him thought she might toss a shoe at his face or make a scene, but she didn't do any of those things.

Truth be told, their relationship had died eight months ago when Cinnamon had randomly called at eleven in the evening. He couldn't believe she had the same phone number. Curiosity had gotten the better of him and he answered. Part of him wished he hadn't. She'd meant to call her cousin, JW. Through her sobs, she apologized profusely and then hung up. It prompted him to call JW the next morning. What he'd learned about Cinnamon's marriage had nearly destroyed him, but there wasn't anything he could do about it. When he tried calling Cinnamon back, she sent him to voicemail. He didn't dare leave a message. He understood what that might cause.

He did, however, text her a few times. It was under the pretense of Whiskey Ranch business. She was still a member of the Whiskey family and she had a stake in the ranch. The few texts he received didn't make much sense. They either had nothing to do with his questions, like how was she? Did she need help? Could they talk? Instead, she said things like she'd gotten her nails done. Or she colored her hair. It was as if she were talking with a girlfriend.

That's when he realized Cinnamon was in big trouble, but he couldn't do anything about it, except talk to her cousins.

His heart had always belonged to Cinnamon. He'd tried to forget her, but he couldn't. Being back at Whiskey Ranch only made him want to see her more. But that was never going to happen and he had to accept it, so he'd poured his soul into ignoring the fact his fiancée was cheating on him.

Big mistake.

And now that was over.

Time to pick up the pieces of his life.

Charity turned on her heel and took one step. She glanced over her shoulder. "On second thought, you can sleep on the sofa."

He chuckled. "And why is that?"

She jerked her chin toward the stable. "That guy over there is always trying to chat me up. He gives me the creeps."

"Gage? He's harmless. But if you're really that wigged out, lock the doors."

"No. You can do this one last favor for me." She cocked her head. "Don't make me beg."

"Fine. But I want you gone tomorrow. We're not playing games. This is over."

"No shit." She flipped her hair and marched off, nearly tripping twice before she even reached the corral's end.

Three weeks later…

Austin lowered his sunglasses. A dark sedan and the local sheriff's vehicle were parked outside his house on the Whiskey Ranch. He tapped his horse's belly with his heels and brought Renegade up to a trot. A steady burn filled his chest and increased as he got closer.

"May I help you?" He dismounted his horse about twenty paces from the police officer and another man dressed in a dark suit. He looked like a government type.

"Are you Austin Sawyer?" the government-looking man asked.

"I am." He thought that was a ridiculous question. "Sheriff Logan, how are you?" He tied Rene-gade to a tree. He'd deal with putting him in the small barn behind the house later.

"I've been better," Brad Logan said. "This is Special Agent Todd Belmont with the FBI."

Austin stretched out his hand. "What brings you gentlemen out here?"

"May we go somewhere and talk?" the Fed asked.

Austin shrugged. "Sure. Come in." He jogged up the stairs and pushed open the front door. "Would you like something to drink? I'm going to get a beer. It's been a long day."

"No, thanks," Brad said.

"I'm good." Belmont nodded.

"Make yourself at home. I'll be right back." Austin's pulse pumped in the center of his throat. He knew exactly why the cops were at his door.

Charity.

He pulled a cold one from the fridge and strolled back into the family room.

The Fed had taken a seat on the wingback chair in front of the fireplace and Brad continued to stand. He looked like he'd swallowed something sour. Good, because Austin and Brad had played football together and he should know that Austin wouldn't have done anything to hurt Charity, no matter the circumstances.

Austin had been in a few barroom fights back in the day, but he'd never lay a hand on a lady.

Not even one who cheated on him.

Austin took a seat on the sofa and swigged. "Why are you here?"

"I need to ask you some questions about the disappearance of your fiancée," Belmont said.

"Ex-fiancée. We broke up the day before she left," Austin corrected. "She was cheating on me with Tom Riptide, whom she returned to Boise to be with." This wasn't the first time someone questioned him about Charity.

Brad had done it once. So had the state police. He'd been on his best behavior both times, but that was before Tom started making wild accusations about his character and telling anyone who would listen that he believed Austin had killed Charity.

Bullshit.

Of course, he knew he shouldn't be so antagonistic with a federal agent, but this was getting out of hand. He'd done nothing wrong.

"But she never made it to Boise." Belmont took out a pen and notepad. "You were the last one to see her alive."

"That's not true and you know it." Austin took another sip of his beverage before setting it on the end table and leaning forward. He hated this game and was tired of playing it. "I helped her pack her car and watched her drive from this house. Two other people at Whiskey Ranch have made official statements with the state police that they saw her after I did. You also have witnesses at a gas station and a credit card record that prove she left this ranch." He held up his hand when Belmont opened his mouth. "I was here at the Whiskey Ranch, doing my job. My boss has stated that fact, as well as others. We can go find them and you can talk to them if you'd like."

"That won't be necessary. I have all their statements." Belmont rested his hand on his pad. "Your story for that first twelve or so hours checks out. But here's where it gets confusing." He licked his finger and flipped the pages backward. "Charity called Tom when she was gassing up her vehicle. She stated that she would stop and have a drink with her friend Cathy."

"Cathy is her best friend. I'm not surprised she'd want to spend time with her and tell her about everything that happened."

"But you know she never made it to meet Cathy." Belmont scanned his handy little notebook.

"I'm aware of that fact." Austin nodded.

"Here's the thing. Most people sleep and Boise isn't that far away. You could have left in the middle of the night and returned by morning." Belmont arched a brow. "Are you going to tell me that's not possible?"

"I didn't leave the ranch."

"But you can't prove it," Belmont said, not giving him a chance to respond, which was probably a good thing, because he had no proof. "Are you also aware Cathy has told us that Charity was afraid of you?"

"No and that's also not true." Austin and Cathy had never liked each other, so it shouldn't be a surprise that she'd go along with all the bullshit Tom was putting out in the universe.

"Cathy said that Charity called her on more than one occasion, crying that you'd gone into a rampage. Throwing things around the house. Yelling and screaming at her. That she was afraid you were actually going to *do it* this time," Belmont said.

"Do what?" Austin asked.

"Kill her." Belmont set his pad back on his lap.

"None of those things ever happened. I never once threatened her. You can ask our neighbors in Boise. And you can ask all the people who live here at Whiskey Ranch."

"Oh, I intend to." Belmont nodded.

"I hope you're looking into Tom as hard as you are me," Austin said under his breath.

"I'm not going to get into that with you." Belmont stood. "Aren't you the least bit concerned about your fiancée?"

"She's my ex and yes, of course I am. I'm very worried, but I didn't do anything except break up with her because she cheated on me. That's it. And I believe that's a reasonable response to the situation." He rose.

"I don't disagree, but sometimes things get out of hand and I've heard you can have quite a temper."

"That was when I was in high school and college. Not to mention I never raised my voice, much less a fist to a woman." Austin let out a long breath. "If you're looking into my past, then I'm sure Sheriff Logan here can tell you that every single time something happened, it was defending the honor of a lady, which includes my mother."

"He's mentioned what kind of man this

community thinks you are, but that doesn't change the fact that a woman is missing and you had motive and opportunity." Belmont lifted his hand. "I'm following every lead. Questioning everyone. You are not a suspect but a person of interest."

Austin understood that wasn't much of a distinction and people had already started to look at him differently. Fear had crept into the eyes of those who didn't know him well and even those who did had that look of wonder.

The damage had been done.

"I want to find out what happened to Charity. I am happy to do whatever is necessary," Austin said.

"I'm glad to hear that." Belmont headed to the front door. "I'm going to have to ask you not to leave the area."

"That won't be a problem." Austin opened the door.

Brad lingered inside while Belmont strolled to his vehicle.

"Jesus. You just stood there like an idiot. You could have defended me a little bit." Austin double-timed it across the room and snatched up his beer. He downed half of it.

"No. I couldn't. At least not while he was questioning you. I have to remain impartial. But I did go through your juvie record and the few fights you got into in college with him, which honestly makes you look like a hothead," Brad said. "However, while I did that, I explained the situation."

"Are you fucking kidding me? That all had to do with my mother and my sister's ex-husband. That bastard beat the fuck of Tina for four years and there wasn't anything I could do about it but hit him back. So I did until she finally left him."

"Thank you for that."

Austin still couldn't get over the fact that his big sister married Brad Logan, of all people. Granted, they didn't come any better than Brad, and he was happy for the two of them, but it was still weird to have one of his best friends from high school as a brother-in-law.

"And for the record, I told Agent Belmont that there was no way in hell you did anything to Charity. That said, I'm still a cop and I have to—"

"Save the explanation. I get it." Austin understood what Brad's position required. Brad had been the one who informed him of Charity's disappearance and what that meant for Austin. "I'm just pissed because Tom gave a press conference the other day and he stated that he believes I murdered her because I went on some jealous rampage. It's fucking laughable. The moment I found out about the affair, I realized I wasn't in love with her."

"But you moved her out here anyway all while you're still in love with Cinnamon."

"Don't bring her into this. She has nothing to do with the breakup."

"That's bullshit and don't try to tell me that you didn't move back here in hopes of seeing her if she were to ever visit so you can help her leave that dick of a man she married." Brad inched closer, waving his finger. "I know you and the one thing you can't tolerate is an abusive man. Even if you didn't care for Cinnamon anymore, you'd want to save her. It's in your DNA and not just because of Tina."

Austin didn't need to be reminded of his shit father and what he'd done to his mother. He watched it. Lived it. Nothing was worse than getting a phone call while at college and learning your mother had been beaten to death. It had changed his world, especially since he thought his father had been out of the picture. His mom had promised she wouldn't let him back in the house. However, his dad could be charming and she'd caved to his apologies and believed he'd turned over a new leaf.

Again.

"Cinnamon won't even talk to me; trust me, I've

tried." He stared at his longtime friend. "I'm terri-fied about what might have happened to Charity and I feel responsible. I should have helped her move back to Boise. Maybe if I had done things differently, she wouldn't be missing."

"You didn't do anything wrong." Brad rested his hand on Austin's shoulder. "Everyone who knows you, believes that. But you have to stop being so combative with the authorities. I know you don't trust us."

"I have good reason not to have faith in most of you." He raked a hand across the top of his head. "My mother called the cops how many times? And so did Tina. But that didn't help them."

"I'm not going to defend my department on why their hands were tied so many times with them, and so many others. Domestic violence is always tough, especially when the victims keep returning to their abusers and change their stories." Brad held up his hand. "I love your sister and I know firsthand what she went through. I hate that my colleagues often had to walk away. I resent that I've been called to homes cider have had to do the same thing. I also can't stand that your good name is being dragged through the mud. But I need you to have a calmer, nicer tone when talking with the Feds. They won't be going away anytime soon."

Austin let out a long breath. "I can do that."

"Good." Brad nodded. "Will you be coming over for dinner? Tina is worried about you."

"I'll be there."

"All right. I need to get back to work. See you in a few hours." Brad turned on his heel and headed out the door.

Austin plopped back on the sofa and pulled out his cell. He found Cinnamon's phone number. He always texted, never called, because when she did respond, it was obvious she couldn't talk. "Fuck it." He tapped the screen. When it rang, he expected it to go right to voicemail. But it didn't. His pulse increased.

Three rings.

"Hello?" Cinnamon's voice came over the speaker soft and sweet.

"Hi, Cinnamon, it's Austin."

"You shouldn't be calling me," she said.

"Why not?" He set his drink on the end table and pinched the bridge of his nose. "We're old friends and I just want to catch up. You know I moved back to the ranch, right?"

"I heard you were engaged. Congratulations."

"Not anymore and unless you live under a rock, I'm sure you've heard what happened." He didn't need to say more.

"What do you want?" Cinnamon asked with a tremor in her voice.

That was a loaded fucking question, and one he wasn't sure he knew how to answer. "All I've ever wanted was for you to be happy and safe and I'm not sure either of those things are true based on the weird texts I get from you." He dropped his head to the sofa and closed his eyes. "Come back to the ranch. It's where you belong."

"I belong with my husband."

He blinked. Anger filled his heart. It pumped through his veins like a wildfire. He knew better than to lecture her about what an asshole Pete was and how she deserved better. That never worked with his mother or with Tina. "Why don't you come for a visit."

"To see you? I don't think so." Her words were laced with the same fury she had the day she told him to fuck off fifteen years ago.

The last year of their relationship had been hard. After his mother had been murdered and his father went to prison, he'd thought about dropping out of college. However, Cinnamon had pushed him to continue his education. She believed it would be good for him to go on with his life. It took a few months, but in the end, he agreed and was happy he'd listened. But then his father died by suicide. He wouldn't have cared had his dad not left a note, blaming him for everything that had happened. His father had rattled off everything Austin had done, including being born, that ruined his life and marriage. Had it not been for Austin, perhaps his mother would still be alive.

Austin knew none of it was true, but it affected him deeply and changed who he was at his core for a long time. Looking back, he could understand why Cinnamon broke up with him, but he could never comprehend how she could fall into the arms of Pete so quickly.

That broke his heart.

"Not me. Your family," he said. "Everyone is worried about you."

"I've got to go. Don't call or text me again. My husband wouldn't appreciate it." The line went dead.

And so did his soul.

1

One year later…

Cinnamon Cider Whiskey set her suitcase and duffel bag on the front porch and pounded on the door. She glanced over her shoulder; fear still had a death grip on her emotions. It didn't matter that Pete had been arrested. He wouldn't stay there forever. He would hire a good lawyer and he'd be out by morning. The worst part was he'd know exactly where to come looking, which is why she wasn't knocking on any of her cousins' doors.

Nope.

She had to pick her ex-boyfriend.

But she didn't know where else to turn and if anyone on this planet would understand, it was Austin.

She glanced at her watch.

One in the morning.

Shit. He was sure to be in bed. She knocked again. Louder this time.

"Who the hell is out there?" Austin called from inside. His voice was raspy and laced with frustration.

"It's Cinnamon. Open the door, please."

The wood barrier opened.

"What the hell?" Austin stood there in a pair of flannel pajama bottoms and nothing else. His dark hair was ruffled from sleep. It was longer than she remembered, touching the back of his neck. "What on earth are you doing here and why are you wearing sunglasses?"

"I'm sure I don't have to explain that one." She pointed to her bags. "Can I crash on your sofa tonight?" The memories of the past bombarded her brain.

Their first kiss. Their first official date. Prom. Visiting him in college. Making love for the first time. The fights. His moods after his father died.

And then fucking Pete.

A guttural sob stuck in her throat.

Austin reached out and gently removed her glasses.

The shame and horror of her life filled her heart. She turned away.

He let out a long breath. "Jesus," he muttered, taking her chin with his thumb and forefinger.

Tears burned the torn skin on her cheeks. The excuses for what happened rushed through her mind. Pete hadn't always been an abuser. He'd been a sweet man when they first got together. However, that had all been a manipulation. Part of his master plan to take her and keep her to himself. He might not have hit her for the first four years of their marriage, but he controlled her in other ways. And he'd never loved her. Not the way a husband should. He married her because she'd been pregnant with the one thing he wanted more than anything.

A child.

Someone to carry on the family name. A little person he could mold and shape into an exact replica of himself.

But when Rosy died, Pete changed. He blamed Cinnamon and when she couldn't get pregnant again, he started beating her. It wasn't all the time, but as the years passed, it worsened. Cinnamon had enough. Pete couldn't ever get past the loss of their little girl and he wanted a son in the worst way. He'd never go to counseling and his fists continued to land on Cinnamon's face.

It was time to put an end to the insanity.

"Come in." Austin stepped aside and then snagged her bags. "Where's Pete?" he asked with a tight tone.

"In jail, for now."

"That's a good place for him." Austin set her luggage by the front bedroom.

She knew this cabin well. A family friend had once occupied it. It had two bedrooms, a family room, and a kitchen. It was located at the north end of the ranch near the bull riding school. Those living in it usually taught lessons or worked at the breeding stables.

Austin had gone to school to study Equine Science. He wanted to be involved in the care and treatment of horses and ranch management. He'd grown up on Whiskey Ranch and intended to return and work there—with her. But that dream was destroyed the day she got pregnant.

She could never say Rosy had been a mistake.

She loved her daughter and cherished every second she had with Rosy. For three years she and Pete had made a decent life. But it hadn't lasted. She missed the ranch. Her family.

And Austin.

"I don't need an *I told you so*."

"I'm not saying that." He planted his hands on his hips. "But those black eyes, the fat lip, and your limp make it hard not to be glad that man is behind bars."

"We both know he'll be out soon enough and he's going to come looking for me. The first place will be at JW's. Or maybe Georgia Moon and Luke's. I just need a night or two to figure out my next move, and then I'll be gone."

"Do any of your cousins know you left?"

"I'll call them in the morning."

"Do you need ice? That swelling is pretty bad."

"It's fine. The cops made me go to the hospital." She stepped around him, making her way into the family room. The furniture had changed since the last time she'd been in this particular cabin. Tired from the evening's horrid events, she plopped herself on the sofa. She groaned, grabbing her midsection.

Austin rushed to her side. Gently, he brushed her hand away and lifted her shirt.

"That motherfucker," he mumbled.

Tears filled her eyes.

"Did he stab you? I counted eighteen stitches." Austin adjusted her shirt. He lifted her chin with his thumb and forefinger and examined her face. "You're limping something awful. Do you have more stitches in your leg?"

"I don't want to talk about this now."

"You don't get to show up at my house in the middle of the night, tell me that your husband is in jail for beating you, and not expect me to ask questions, especially when you know my history with domestic violence."

"I thought you of all people would understand and not grill me."

"For fuck's sake, Cinnamon. That's not what I'm doing. I want to know what happened. What's been happening. Ever since you called me over a year ago, I've been worried sick about you. I know your cousins have all been trying to get you to leave that asshole for years." He pressed his finger gently over her bruised lip. "I do get that it's not easy. I understand the hold an abuser has over their victims. This is not your fault. But now that you've taken the first step, you have to do the hard part and stick with it."

"You don't get to tell me what I need to do. You left me years ago." She closed her eyes. She'd told herself on the ride over she wouldn't get into this conversation with Austin. It wasn't the right time or place. What happened between them was long ago and she had no right to still be angry. It was childish and stupid.

This wasn't his fault either.

But sometimes it was easier to blame him because deep down she still loved him.

"I know you're hurting and if you want to take it out on me, go ahead," he said.

She blinked. "No. I'm sorry. It's just, you have no idea what my life has been like since my daughter died."

Austin wrapped his arms around her and pulled her to his chest. He pressed his lips against her forehead.

It felt like home.

"I'm so sorry about Rosy. I felt like the worst human when I found out. I was such an ass for not staying in touch with anyone at the ranch. If I had known about her passing, I would have reached out.

I was a jerk and caught up in my own hurt feelings."

She rested her head against his strong shoulder. For the first time in a long while, she felt safe. It was as if the past fifteen years melted away, except for the pain of losing her precious baby. That could never be erased. "I never meant to hurt you. I was young and scared. You changed after your dad died and I reacted badly."

"I was a fool not to fight for you." He ran his hands up and down her arms. "We can't do anything about the past. What's done is done. But you can't go back to Pete."

"I know. He's out of control. He won't go to counseling and things have gotten really bad. I'm done trying to make things right. He can't see beyond his own misery and he takes it out on me. I won't be his punching bag anymore. I filed for divorce, which provoked this beating in the first place."

"Why didn't you have an exit plan? You were there when I helped Tina do that."

She glanced up. "You know how shameful this is and I'm tired of hearing how I need to leave him. I know my family means well, but everyone has an opinion and I don't want to be a burden."

He brushed his lips across her temple. "Your cousins only wish to help. However, you've pushed them away. JD told me a couple of weeks ago that you barely take their phone calls and you didn't come back to the ranch for the holidays."

There were so many reasons she'd avoided her family. However, the moment Pete learned Austin was back at the ranch, there was no way she'd ever be allowed to return again. Besides, knowing he lived on Whiskey Ranch changed everything. It stirred her emotions in ways she couldn't deal with, at least not while she was still married to Pete.

Nor while Austin was engaged to another woman.

And there was the fact that Charity was still missing and the rumors that haunted Austin's good name.

"You know why I did all those things." She pushed from his embrace. She didn't want to get too comfortable. Her life was too complicated to allow any past emotions to clutter her difficult situation. "For years, you never brought friends home because of what went on in your house."

"That's different. I was a kid."

She arched a brow. "Do you still do volunteer work with battered women?"

He nodded.

"Then you know it's never easy for someone to leave and not just because of the emotional hold the abuser has over their victims." She stood, lifting her shirt, twisting her body, showing off the other stab wound. "I have one more on my leg with twelve stitches and this isn't the first time he's stabbed me. He's also bought a gun. I'm terrified he'll come here and hurt my cousins or their children. Or you. He hates you."

"The feeling is more than mutual." Austin folded his arms across his chest and scowled. "The security on the ranch is excellent and I'll call my brother-in-law in the morning. We'll make sure everyone, including you, is well protected."

"That's not my point and you know it."

He stood, gripping her biceps. "We may not have seen each other in fifteen years, but I think you know me well enough to know I'm not going to stand here and let that man hurt you again."

"It's that tone that makes me wonder if I made the right decision to come to you."

He chuckled.

"I'm serious. You have a wicked temper sometimes."

"I have only ever hit three men, and they all

deserved it." He lowered his chin. "Including Pete because he swung first."

"You were acting like a jealous idiot."

Austin took a step back. "He knocked up my girlfriend. What did you expect me to do?"

"Oh my God. First, it takes two people to make a baby. Second, I wasn't your girlfriend at the time."

"Well, I came home to make things right between us and he tells me you're pregnant and then pulls out a ring and proposes right in front of me like you're some damned trophy or something." Austin raked a hand over the top of his head. "I get I was being pigheaded and acting like a jerk, but he was a total dick and sucker punched me. All I did was call him a fucking douchebag with no class."

"You told him he was going to be a shit father and offered to raise the baby as your own."

"And I would have if you'd let me." His chest heaved in as he sucked in a deep breath. "Fuck. I don't want to fight with you about this. It's all in the past and you've got enough to deal with."

"You're right, so I don't need you throwing a punch."

"I won't promise you anything about that," he muttered. "Any man who puts a hand on a lady is scum in my book." He marched toward the front bedroom. "There are clean sheets on the bed. I'll put your things in the room. I'm in the room behind the kitchen. If you need anything at all, don't hesitate to wake me. I'll be up by dawn. I'm sure I can rearrange my work schedule."

"I don't want you to do that for me."

He squeezed her shoulder. "You're here now, so let me help."

"Thank you."

He kissed her forehead. "Try to get some sleep. I'll see you in the morning." He closed the door behind him, leaving her in the bedroom alone.

The tears came hot and fast.

She'd made a mess of her life and she was only thirty-four years old. Rummaging through her suitcase, she found her pajamas and carefully slipped them on. Her entire body was covered in bruises. She ached from head to toe. The stab wounds hadn't done any real damage, thank God. She'd been lucky Pete had been so drunk he could barely stand. That had been the only reason she'd been able to get away. She'd locked herself in the bathroom and called the police.

But Pete had managed to bust down the door. That's when he attacked her with the knife. The cops arrived just as he stabbed her in the thigh, finally giving her the witnesses she needed to press charges. Pete wouldn't be able to get away with it this time. He'd face real prison time and she would be strong and hold him accountable for his actions. She was done playing the victim.

After brushing her teeth, she found her cell charger. The nurse at the hospital had reminded her to turn off her location, but suggested she get a new cell. She'd do that tomorrow. For now, she felt secure that Pete couldn't track the device. As soon as she lifted it from her purse, she noticed ten missed calls and twenty texts.

All from Pete.

Her heart dropped like a cement brick.

He was out already.

2

*A*ustin climbed into bed and stared at the ceiling.

Cinnamon was back and the first thing he'd done was pick a fight. Or maybe she had, but it didn't matter. They were right back to where they'd been fifteen years ago. There was so much unresolved conflict between them, and there shouldn't be any issues anymore.

They both had made their choices.

"Austin." Cinnamon came barreling into his room. She stood at the side of his bed with tears rolling down her battered face.

Rage filled his veins. If he ever saw Pete again, someone would have to restrain him because he couldn't control himself.

He bolted upright. "What's wrong?"

She held her phone out. "It's Pete. Someone bailed him out."

"In the middle of the night? How the hell did that happen?"

"I don't know, but he has a lot of wealthy friends in high places. He's been trying to reach me for the last hour. He's left nasty voice and text messages."

"Can I see?" He reached for the phone.

"Sure."

He patted the side of his bed. "Sit down. Try to relax. I know it's hard, but you're safe here."

"I'm not safe anywhere with him out of jail and those messages prove it."

Austin started with the texts.

Pete: *You bitch. I can't believe you did this to me. I will get you for this. And if you think these stupid charges will stick, you've got another thing coming.*

Pete: *Answer your damn phone.*

Pete: *Where the fuck are you? How dare you turn off your location. You think I won't find you? As if there are a ton of places you'd go? You're probably back in Buhl. Ha. If you think your idiot cousins can keep you from me, think again.*

Pete: *You fucking little whore. I know who's back at*

Whiskey Ranch. You think I'm a monster? He killed his fiancée. He'll do the same to you because you're damaged goods. I'm the only one who will ever want you. I'll give you a day to come home, and then I'm coming to get you.

Pete: *Pick up the damned phone, you little cunt. I'm tired of this game. You're never going to leave me. You like my money too much. Fucking bitch. Get your ass home now and make sure these cops drop the charges. If you don't, you'll pay.*

Austin had read enough. He set the phone on the other side of the bed. He certainly didn't want Cinnamon to read or listen to any more from Pete. It would only stress her out. "I'm going to call Brad now." He reached for his phone.

"I don't want you to wake him or Tina up. Don't they have a newborn?"

"Gabby's one and Ben is four." He tapped his screen. "Neither one of them will care if I call about this. Besides, I'm not risking that Pete will wait a day or two to show his face in Buhl. He's irrational and this is harassment. Brad and his department need to know. The next call we are making is to JW."

"Absolutely not." She jumped to her feet. "I will deal with my family on my own terms."

"It's almost two in the morning," Brad said when he picked up on the second ring. "What's wrong?"

"It's Cinnamon. She left Pete after he beat the crap out of her. He was in jail but has since been bailed out and is now sending her threatening messages. I'll text you screenshots."

"Do that now so I can take a look."

Austin did as instructed and waited.

"Does she have a restraining order in place? If she doesn't, we can file one here just in case."

"Let's do that."

"All right. She'll need to sign it," Brad said. "I can bring that by first thing."

"Wonderful, but I think the ranch needs a little extra security."

"I'll make sure units are patrolling the entrances," Brad said. "I'll see you in the morning."

"Thanks." He tapped the screen and pulled up JW's contact information.

"I swear to God, I'll walk out that front door if you call any of my cousins." She groaned when she folded her arms across her middle. "I'm not ready to face them."

"Ready or not, they have a right to know that he

could be on his way here. Not to mention they love you and only want you to be safe. That's all they care about." He stared at her for a long moment. "Is there something else you're not telling me?"

She turned, swiping at her cheeks.

He climbed from the bed. "Cinnamon. What's going on?" Gently, he took her by the arms, forcing her to face him. "Whatever it is, I can't help unless you tell me."

"A few months before you moved back, Pete and I visited the ranch. It ended badly."

"I heard."

"I doubt they told you everything, especially Irish." She shrugged off his embrace and crawled into his bed, hugging his pillow. "It was a real shit show. At first, I had planned on coming by myself. Pete hates this place."

"I remember. He moved you away from Buhl the second you got married, and according to Georgia Moon, you barely came back."

"At first, Pete had me convinced the only way we had a shot at a real marriage was if we had a clean break from everyone. I believed him because my family all believed I was making a mistake. They didn't think being pregnant was the right reason to marry someone. Not to mention, all Pete ever wanted was to work for his father and when I got pregnant, his dad offered him a job."

Austin had wanted to interject, but kept his mouth shut.

"I was so focused on being a good mom and wife that I was okay with it. Things weren't great, but I had Rosy. Then my baby girl got sick. She was only two years old. The next year was fucking hell."

"I can't even imagine." Austin eased in next to Cinnamon and rested his arm around her hip.

"Both Pete and I were devastated. Believe it or not, he was a devoted dad. He loved his little girl. She was his world. He would have done anything for her and for a few short years, we were happy-ish."

"It's the ish part that bothers me."

She let out a dry laugh. "Pete and I never truly loved each other, but Rosy brought us close. Her death sent Pete into a downward spiral that was compounded by my inability to get pregnant again." The tears poured out of her eyes like a waterfall. "I didn't want to start trying again so soon, but Pete was relentless. That's when he started hitting me."

Austin reined in his anger. He wondered what else might have happened and couldn't allow his brain to go there. The guilt he felt was too strong. He'd let down the only woman he'd ever loved and he loathed himself for it.

"Every time I had to tell him I wasn't pregnant, he'd slap me. It wasn't bad at first."

"Don't make excuses for his bad behavior."

"You know how this works." She squeezed the pillow. "We were both in a bad place. I had been seeing a therapist but couldn't get him to go. I tried giving him an ultimatum. Either he went or I was going to leave, and that's when things took a really bad turn. I stopped going to counseling."

"You stopped, or he decided for you?"

"I didn't want to fight him or get hit, so I didn't go anymore. I also avoided my family even more. It was a really dark time. Anyway, when we came here the last time, everyone was trying to get me to leave him. Every second someone had me alone, they'd start talking exit strategies. The pressure was insurmountable. But it was Irish who got in my face. Pete overheard us. He was livid. The fight between him and Irish was something I will never forget."

"Irish told me about it," Austin admitted. "He said that you left in the middle of the night, but he wasn't sure if you went willingly or not and that you haven't spoken to anyone since, except the one time you accidentally called me."

"I did not want to go. Pete woke me up and told me that if I fought him on this, he'd make sure my family was ruined."

"He's tried to do that before. He's never been successful."

"Pete's family has money. Lots of it."

"I'm well aware." That had always been a bone of contention with Austin. He'd listened to whispers around town about how Cinnamon had run off with Pete because he could give her more than a broken cowboy with a questionable past and not even two nickels to rub together. Deep down, he didn't want to believe it, but some days it was hard.

"They have a lot of power in this state. Pete has done and said things to undermine my family business. If I stay away, he leaves them alone. When I contact anyone in my family, he stirs the pot. He'll call anyone he can think of and send them out here."

"We were pretty sure he was the one who caused all the trouble for Kitty and the educational facility two years ago."

Cinnamon nodded. "Pete has cut me off from my family and my friends. I only want a few days to figure things out, and then I'm leaving. I can't put my family at risk. Do you understand?"

"Yes and no." Austin leaned back and stared at the fan. "I get you want to protect everyone, but they want to do the same for you. Besides, Pete can't hurt them because they aren't doing anything wrong. He can send all the inspectors and anyone else he wants. Everything at Whiskey Ranch is on the up-and-up and you know that. Running from this is only putting yourself at risk. You're staying put. I won't be the only one who feels that way. So let me call your cousins."

"They don't want to hear from me." She sniffled. "My last words with Irish and JD weren't pleasant. They told me I had to leave Pete."

"I believe their words were to call them when you were ready." He turned his head, arching a brow. "You forget that JD and I were once best friends and we've rekindled that friendship. I got the entire story when I moved back and Charity moved out. I doubt they left anything out and they did say they were harsh, something they've regretted. However, tough love is sometimes necessary."

"Looks like you've returned to your logical self." She curled up next to him, wrapping her arm around his middle and draping a leg over his knee.

"The last time we were together, you acted like a moron."

"I was angry and hurt."

"So was I," she said.

"It's all in the past. All that matters now is making sure Pete doesn't ever hurt you again." He waved his phone. "I'm calling JW now."

"Okay." She sighed. "Pete's not going to go away quietly."

"I know. But you have an entire family who will be by your side. You're not alone in this."

"I'm sorry that I dumped my problems at your feet. I should have been brave enough to go to my family to begin with."

"Don't be silly." He kissed her temple. "I watched my mother and sister go through what you're living. It makes sense that you'd come to me first."

She lifted her head. "Not with our history it doesn't."

Setting his cell on the mattress, he took her chin with his thumb and forefinger. "No matter what happened between us, I never stopped caring about you. I'm glad you felt you could come to me. You can stay here as long as you want or need to."

"You're a kind man, Austin."

He should either ask her to go back to the guest room or leave himself, but he didn't have the self-control to do either. Instead, he held her in his arms while he made the difficult phone call to JW.

"What the hell are you doing calling me at two in the morning?" JW asked with a gruff voice.

Austin quickly went through the details. JW cussed on the other end.

"No. It's not necessary for you to come over now," Austin said. "She's sleeping." It was only a half lie as Cinnamon's breathing slowed and exhaustion overtook her body.

"I can't believe she went to you and not one of us," JW muttered.

Austin lifted the sheets and comforter over their bodies and clicked the light off. "I could give you a thousand reasons why, but none of them matter. She's filed for divorce and she's here at the ranch."

"But you said he's out on bail. That doesn't make me feel good about the situation. I've seen firsthand what that asshole can do."

Austin wasn't about to tell JW how badly Pete had beaten Cinnamon. "Brad's in contact with the Boise police. If he shows up, Brad can arrest him. Pete's in a shitload of trouble. Don't worry. I'll keep a watchful eye on her tonight. And we can all take turns until Pete is behind bars for good."

"How are you doing with this?"

Austin lowered his gaze. In the dark, he could barely see Cinnamon. Her head rested on his chest. Her hair was draped across his body. "I'm just glad she's home where she belongs."

Cinnamon sat on the main house front porch where her cousin JW Whiskey and his lovely wife, Kitty, lived. Their two toddlers, Cheye and Manny, ran around the front yard. It brought so many emotions to Cinnamon's soul. She missed her little girl so badly. Rosy would have been fourteen. Hard to believe.

"Here you go." Kitty handed her a tall glass of lemonade. She eased into one of the Adirondack chairs and sipped her beverage.

Cinnamon had only met Kitty once and it hadn't been under the best of circumstances. "Your kids are so adorable."

"They're on their best behavior today, but trust me, they can sometimes be holy terrors." Kitty brushed her red hair from her face. "I don't know if Austin or JW told you any of what I went through with my ex-husband."

"Only that your ex had done some shady things."

"That's an understatement." Kitty laughed. "It was a difficult time and there were moments that I wasn't sure I'd get through it." She leaned forward. "I don't pretend to understand what you're going through. My ex-husband hit me once. His abuse was more emotional. However, I'm happy to listen if you ever want a girl to chat with. I know how overpowering, though well meaning, some of your male cousins can be."

"That's putting it mildly." Cinnamon raised her glass. "I feel lighter now that everyone knows I've left, filed for divorce, and am here. But it's all nerve-racking now that Pete's been bailed out and no one has seen him since then. I worry he's lurking in some bush, waiting to attack."

"We have hired extra security and JD, JB, Luke, and Irish are all installing more cameras around the ranch as we speak. No one will get on the property without us knowing about it."

"Not to mention I don't think Austin will leave my side." Cinnamon wasn't sure what to do about that. She appreciated his concern and she was the one to go to him for help. Her feelings for him had never died. Waking in his bed, alone, had been both a blessing and a curse. She would have wanted to kiss him, and maybe more if he'd been there.

That's the last thing she needed.

This entire mess began because she'd jumped into bed with Pete before things had truly ended with Austin. The cause and effect of her actions had always left her with a major moral dilemma. She couldn't wish her daughter away. She'd never regret those three beautiful years.

However, in some ways, it had robbed her of a life with Austin.

Maybe.

She'd never know now.

"Or Gage." Kitty pointed to the handyman working on the fence in the distance. "When he heard you were going to be here this morning, he asked if he could work on the fence versus other projects."

Cinnamon laughed. Some people found Gage to be an odd man. And maybe he was a little. He'd always had a fondness for her and followed her around like a little lovesick puppy. The few times she'd come home, he'd shown up with handpicked flowers. It was a sweet gesture, one that Pete hated and he'd let Gage know. Pete treated Gage like he was a weirdo or a pervert.

Whereas Austin accepted Gage's kindness and often encouraged it. Gage would nod and smile and say, *Yes, Mr. Sawyer. I understand. I just want to make the ladies here smile.*

And that's what Gage did. It wasn't just Cinnamon who got special treatment from Gage. It was everyone. He was a kind man who had lost his family in a tragic fire. He'd always been a bit odd, even before his family died. However, there was a story there and if anyone had ever cared to sit down and chat with Gage, they'd understand why he was different.

"He's such a sweet old man," Cinnamon said.

"When I first moved to the ranch, he used to bring me daisies every day. He'd tell me what a bitch JW's ex-fiancée Bella was and how I brightened up the place. Now he brings the kids little toys every couple of weeks. I wish I could tell him to stop because he's spoiling them, but it's not like they are expensive. Half the time they are handmade."

"His story makes me want to cry," Cinnamon said. "The way his family died and all. His daughter Ashley was like him—on the spectrum. She was my friend and it always made me sad the way others often treated her."

"He's made this ranch his home. I just wish more people treated him better." Kitty sighed. "Austin's ex-fiancée was such a mean girl. I hate to say it, but I was thrilled when she left and Gage did a little jig when she drove that fancy car that Austin had bought her away. But now he feels guilty because we still have no idea what happened to her. It haunts Austin."

"I can't understand how anyone would believe he could kill a person." Cinnamon shook her head. "Although, I did watch him beat the crap out of his dad and his ex-brother-in-law once. It wasn't a pretty sight and it's a side of him I never want to see again."

"I forgot the two of you were an item."

"We started dating—if you could call it that— when I was twelve and he was fourteen. We broke up when I was nineteen. Right before I married Pete. But even when Austin and I were in grade school, we were attached at the hip. He was my best friend before he became my boyfriend. Losing him was one of the hardest things—outside of the death of my daughter—that I've ever gone through."

"You know, if it's too weird to stay with him, you're welcome here with JW and me."

"Thank you. JB told me the same thing. But everyone has little kids and if Pete does manage to get on the ranch, I wouldn't want to expose any of the children to his craziness. For now, I'll remain at the cabin with Austin." Cinnamon had given a lot of consideration to JB and Cheyenne's offer. Being so close to Austin made her want to forget the last fifteen years. Her heart ached to be with him in ways she didn't understand, nor did she want to examine.

The drive from Idaho Falls to Buhl had been filled with thoughts of the past mixed with emotions she didn't know she had. At first, she chalked it up to the idea she hadn't seen Austin in fifteen years, but the second she laid eyes on him, the love she had felt for him all those years ago flooded her heart. It was as if it had been hidden in a vault and leaving Pete had been the key to unlocking it.

However, her battle had just begun.

Even with the charges that Pete faced, he wasn't going to let her go easily. Pete didn't like to lose and he viewed her as a trophy.

"That man has been through a lot," Kitty said. "Agent Belmont comes around about once a month,

asking him questions about Charity's disappearance."

"Austin wouldn't ever hurt a woman."

"We know that, but others have painted a very different story."

"Austin mentioned that, but I still struggle with anyone believing that. If they know his history, they'd understand why he could never."

Kitty leaned back and glanced toward the door. "Austin and JW won't be thrilled with me telling you this. If you google it, you'll find articles and blogs about it. There's more out there about him as a potential murderer than there is about the other man whom Charity was involved with." Kitty held up her hand. "It doesn't matter that there have been a few holes poked in Tom's story, not to mention that Tom doesn't really believe Austin did it anymore and that Cathy—a friend of Charity's—had stated she was going to meet Charity for drinks, but the bartender said he never saw Cathy at that bar waiting for her friend. Which is weird, right?"

"It does sound strange, but I honestly haven't read much on the story other than she went missing." Tears burned Cinnamon's dry, swollen eyes. "Pete controlled many things in my life, including the amount of time I spent on the computer and he often took my phone. The last two years were the worst."

Kitty's face hardened. Her lips pursed and she clasped her hands in her lap. "My ex-husband was a controlling bastard. He used his money and power to manipulate me. It wasn't as bad as what you're describing. However, there's one thing I know, having been in that situation, and that is it takes a little space to gather enough courage to be completely done. You can't have any contact with him. If he calls, don't answer, because he's eventually going to change from being a total asshole to being as sweet as a peach."

"Oh, trust me. I know." Cinnamon nodded. "The first time he hit me, he apologized the second it happened. He spent weeks making it up to me. And it didn't happen again for months. He even went to a counseling session. But then something happened and the next time it wasn't a slap; it was a punch in the gut and it took him two days to say he was sorry." She wiped a tear that dribbled down her cheek. "The escalation was slow, but I'm so done. He's so far gone that there is no turning back. Pete's dangerous and I know if I were to ever return, I'd end up in a body bag and that's no way to honor my baby girl's short life."

Kitty reached out and took Cinnamon's hand. "If you ever want someone to talk to, I'm here for you."

"Thanks. I appreciate that." Cinnamon sipped her drink and waved to Gage who smiled and waved back. "I will need to find something to do once I feel a little better and get these stitches out. Otherwise, I'm going to go mad. I can't sit on my ass and do nothing. Pete wouldn't allow me to work and it made me feel like I was useless. I hate that feeling."

"My ex was the same way. When I left, the first thing I did was go back to school." Kitty jerked her head toward the house. "JW and I had a long-distance relationship for a while so I could finish my bachelor's degree. It wasn't easy with me still living in Baltimore, but he was super supportive. And now I have the education facility here at the ranch."

"I've always wanted to be a teacher." More tears burned a path down her face. "I had been going to college locally to become a preschool educator while I waited for Austin to return. But things didn't work out."

"He's never talked about what happened."

Cinnamon chuckled. "That is a long and convoluted story."

"Curiosity killed this Kitty."

"Oh my God. You did not just say that." Cinnamon shook her head. Pete had isolated her from her family. She'd missed all her cousins' weddings. The births of their children. Hell, this was the first time she was meeting some of them. She hated him for taking this away from her and loathed herself for allowing it to happen. "I'll try to break it down into a short tale."

"You don't have to talk about it if you don't want to."

"No. It's okay. But I'm sure my version is a bit different from Austin's."

"That's always the case."

Cinnamon set her drink on the table and let out a long breath while she gathered her thoughts. "When Austin's father died by suicide, it affected him deeply. He always tried to tell himself that he had no feelings for his dad. I kept telling him that he did. That there was a hint of love in his heart. It was his father and his dad did show up to football games. He took him fishing. He never hit Austin until Austin was in college, but that was only because Austin, as an adult, couldn't stand there and let his father beat the crap out of his mom. He was also dealing with his sister who married an abusive man. The cycle had been handed down."

"That's rough."

"The truth was that Austin was afraid he would be like his dad because he does have a temper."

"I've never seen it," Kitty said. "He's always so zen."

Cinnamon laughed. "Trust me. Austin can be jealous and if he sees a wrong when it comes to a woman, he has no problem stepping in. His father refused a plea deal and the case went to trial. Austin had to testify. That was the beginning of our problems because Austin was conflicted. His testimony helped put his father away for twenty years. When his dad died, he left a note blaming Austin. But it wasn't just the blame. The comparison of how they are alike started Austin on this weird path. He pulled away from me. He stopped coming home as often. He broke up with me, and then he'd want me back. I'd end it with him, and then he'd come home and things were good. This went on for almost a year. Meanwhile, I had Pete in my ear, telling me how he'd make for a better boyfriend. He'd buy me lavish gifts and he was always there when I needed him."

"Oh shit," Kitty said. "Sounds like he tossed over a line with the right bait."

"You could say that, but Austin wasn't helping, and one night on the phone, we got into a big fight and I told him to fuck off. That we were done. I saw Pete that night, went to bed with him, and got pregnant. The weird part was that Austin wasn't all that pissed at me when he came home and found out. His rage was directed at Pete."

"Do you think he knew what kind of man Pete was?"

Cinnamon shrugged. "Maybe. He has good radar that way. He offered to raise the baby as his own, but once I decided to marry Pete, Austin walked away and I never heard from him. Not one phone call. Nothing."

"No offense, but what did you expect him to do?"

"I suppose exactly what he did. He felt I had given up on us, but I had been feeling that way for the last year. I was young and stupid and he was pigheaded and hurting over his father. It was a series of events that we—at the time—didn't have the tools to deal with."

"Hindsight is always perfect vision," Kitty said. "How do you feel seeing him now?"

Cinnamon glanced toward the sky. A flock of birds flew overhead. She focused on them for as long as she could while sorting through all the emotions. "So much is going on in my life right now. I'm scared about what Pete will do while he's out awaiting trial because he'll be like Austin's father. He'll fight as if he did nothing wrong. An uncontested divorce in this state only takes sixty-two days, but he'll fight that too, so it could take a while. But I have to admit, I do still have feelings for Austin."

"We all know he cares very deeply for you," Kitty said.

"He's said that?" Cinnamon's heart fluttered like the first time Austin took her hand while they walked across the ranch. She'd been all of twelve. He whispered in her ear about how much he liked her and how pretty she looked.

"Not to me. And I don't know if he's mentioned it to JW or any of your cousins, but ever since he's moved back here, he's always asking if anyone has talked to you or if we knew what was happening with you and Pete. Once, he did it at the dinner table with Charity sitting right next to him." Kitty laughed. "She got up and walked out the door and Austin let her go without saying a word.

That's when we knew he didn't want to be with her."

"How long after that did she leave?"

"Not for another month. We had no idea she'd been cheating on him. He didn't tell us until after she left," Kitty said.

"I wonder why he kept that to himself."

"He told us later it was because he wanted to confront her first. He did that and she left the next day." Kitty sighed. "Sadly, she's been missing for a year. Austin hired a private investigator to look into her disappearance but has found nothing. Gage watched her drive away. She stopped at a gas station not far from here, but after that, no one has seen her or heard from her since."

"That's terrifying."

"There has been no sign of her, but every once in a while, an anonymous tip comes into the Feds, leading them right to Austin," Kitty said. "We truly hope they find her—and that she's okay—but it's not looking good."

"I just wish the spotlight wasn't on Austin. He's a good man with a big heart."

"For the most part, he takes it all in stride, but occasionally, he loses his shit."

"I'm sure he does."

Kitty glanced at her watch. "I hate doing this to you, but I must get to work." She stood. "Hey. I have a great idea. One of the girls in the infant room will be leaving soon on maternity leave and you don't need a degree. I need to be official and do a background check, but I'm happy to hire you as a fill-in if you'd like. The position will open up in a week and I haven't found anyone yet."

"Are you serious?"

"I wouldn't joke about that." Kitty smiled. "It's a temp position. But if you're going to stay at the ranch and would consider going back to school, I might be able to find you a more permanent gig."

Cinnamon had no idea what her future held or even if Whiskey Ranch would be a part of it, much less getting the degree she'd always felt robbed of, but her soul came to life at the thought. "I'd love to take the temp job. How do we go about getting the paperwork started?"

"Come by the education facility when you can. I'll be there most of the day, but my assistant will have it if I'm out. As soon as it's filled out, I'll file it and once I get it back, you can start. It should only take three business days."

"I'll be by later this morning." She rose and hugged Kitty. "Thank you so much."

"Anything for family." She put her forefinger and thumb to her mouth and gave a big whistle. "Let's go, kiddos. Time for school."

Her two children came flying up the porch steps, ran a circle around her legs while giggling, and then raced right through the front door, Kitty following one step behind.

For the first time in a long while, Cinnamon believed her life could actually turn around.

———

Austin leaned against the counter in JW's kitchen and took the cup of coffee that JW offered.

"Well, last night sounds exciting," JW said.

"Not sure that's the word I'd use to describe it." Austin chuckled. "I was a little gobsmacked to see Cinnamon standing on my front stoop at one in the morning, and then it took every ounce of energy I had not to get in my truck and drive to Idaho Falls."

"Knowing you, thoughts of beating the crap out of Pete danced in your head like sugar plums."

"Exactly." Austin nodded in agreement. "If he does show up here, we all better hope he and I don't cross paths because my blood is on fire."

"So is mine." JW filled his mug and pulled back

a stool at the island. "You told me she was in bad shape, but you didn't prepare me for what her face looked like."

"At least she's not making excuses for Pete anymore."

"I can't believe she let it go on this long." JW rubbed the back of his neck. "I'm so mad at myself for not being a better cousin."

"Trust me when I say there's not a lot you could have done. My mom stayed with my dad on and off for nearly twenty-five years. My sister left her first husband because I landed myself in county lockup for beating the shit out of him. Had I not done that, who knows how long she might have stayed before either the worst happened or she had enough. Abuse is tricky, and victims are beaten down emotionally to the point they have no voice."

JW laughed. "I know that's not funny, but I'll never forget me and JD picking you up that morning. You were quite proud of yourself and at the same time, you looked as though you'd swallowed a lemon."

"I should regret my actions. But I don't. And now she's married to Brad, which is still weird as fuck."

"Yeah. They make for an odd couple."

"They're happy and that's all that matters." Austin peered through the house. He wished he could see out the door to the porch. Better yet, he wanted to hear what Kitty and Cinnamon discussed. He was glad Cinnamon was back where she had a major support network.

And protection.

Pete wouldn't last two seconds if he set foot on Whiskey Ranch.

"How are you holding up? It has to be strange to see Cinnamon after all these years," JW said.

"That's the understatement of the century, and yet, in an odd way, it's like no time has passed."

"I have to ask. Why did she go to you and not her family?" JW raised his hand. "Don't get me wrong. I'm simply glad she's here, so it doesn't really matter. But I am a little butt hurt that she didn't feel comfortable coming to me. Or Irish. She's the closest to him."

"Well, I know Irish had some pretty harsh words for her the last time they spoke and as for you or the rest of your siblings, it has more to do with her fear that Pete will come and cause a scene in front of the children. Or worse. Not to mention the shame she feels."

"Damn. I hate that we made her feel that way."

"It's not you. It's the nature of abuse," Austin said. "I lived it my entire life. There were times I thought my dad beat my mom because of me. That if I somehow was a better kid, he wouldn't do it. I know that's crazy, but to a small child, when you hear your father say things like, *you're making our kids pansies,* or *Austin would be a better linebacker if you didn't coddle him so much,* or my all-time favorite, *I'm not even sure I'm their dad.*"

"I can't tell you how many times your dad almost lost his job. The only reason Chuck Holland or my grandparents kept him on was because of you and Tina."

"I'm well aware of that fact and completely grateful for so many reasons. Growing up here gave me so many opportunities." He pointed toward the front door. "One of them is sitting out there. Only I fucked that up royally."

"She made her share of mistakes, like sleeping with Pete."

"I forgave her for that the moment it happened." Austin rubbed his temple. "I wasn't a saint either. I said some horrible things to her the night that happened. Not to mention I slept with someone else too and she knew about it. But she broke my heart when she married that prick. I would have taken care of her and her little girl."

"Watching Rosy die of cancer was the worst. That was the only time we were ever allowed to be part of their lives. I thought for sure she'd leave him and come home. But things went downhill from there."

"I don't think I'll ever forgive myself for cutting all ties to this ranch, this family, or her for so long." Austin downed his coffee in three gulps. It burned his belly. "She says she's done and I believe her. I hope Pete gets what he deserves."

The front door flew open.

"Daddy!" Cheye came running into the kitchen and flung herself at JW. "Mommy says it's time for school."

"Then I guess we better finish getting ready." He leaned over and kissed his little girl on the cheek. "Go upstairs and I'll be there in a second to help you brush your teeth."

"Uncle Austin." Manny tugged at Austin's pant leg. "Look." He held out a frog.

"I don't think your mama would appreciate that thing in her house." Austin laughed.

"No, she would not." JW leaned over and scooped up Manny. "Let's take that out back. Next time you'll go to bed without a snack. Got it, kiddo?"

"Yes, sir." Manny frowned.

Austin bit his lower lip to keep from cracking up.

"What's so funny?" Kitty appeared in the kitchen.

"Absolutely nothing." Austin snagged his Stetson from the table. "Where's Cinnamon?"

"Still sitting on the front porch." Kitty curled her fingers around Austin's biceps. "Please make sure she comes by the educational center today. I offered her a temp job. But also, the deadline to enroll in fall classes at the local college is in three weeks. Encourage her to do it. I know she's hurting and a lot is going on, but the sooner she moves on with her life, the faster she'll heal. It will also help her gain the strength and confidence she needs to get through what's coming next."

Austin kissed Kitty's cheek. "You're a good woman, Kitty Whiskey."

"That has always had such an odd ring to it."

"I used to tease Cinnamon about her name. I mean, come on, Cinnamon Cider Whiskey?" He smacked his forehead. "Have you ever had one of those drinks? They are gross, unlike the woman who bears the name. Speaking of which, I should go. Letting her sit and overthink might not be a good idea."

"Agreed." Kitty smiled. "Call us if you need anything."

He adjusted his hat and headed toward the door. JW and the other cousins decided that Austin would take time off work and stay with Cinnamon. No one wanted her alone and Austin was all too willing to take on the responsibility.

It was the least he could do.

CINNAMON'S BLACKWIDOW

4

———

$\mathcal{A}$ustin leaned against the wall by Cinnamon's bedroom door. The guttural sobs that filtered through the air cut his soul in half. He closed his eyes and clenched his fists. He'd gotten out of bed to get a glass of water. He'd been restless and unable to sleep. He thought he'd heard something and took a walk down the hallway.

Part of him wished he hadn't.

The other part wanted to go in and comfort her, but he had no idea if she'd even welcome it.

Shit. He couldn't stand it a second longer. He tapped at the door. "Cinnamon?" He pushed open the door a crack. "I'm coming in."

"You don't have to." She sniffled. "I'm fine."

"No. You're not. I can hear you halfway down

the hall." He stepped in, leaving the door ajar, allowing the light to filter in.

She was curled up in the bed, hugging a pillow. She pulled the covers over her head. "I'm just having a moment."

Flashes to his childhood filled his mind. His mom used to cry herself to sleep. He couldn't stand that there was nothing he could do to comfort her or make things better. Same for his sister. He'd be damned if he'd let Cinnamon go through this alone.

He strolled to the other side of the bed and pulled back the sheets.

"What are you doing?" She popped her head up.

Wrapping his arms around her, he shifted her body, tucking her head into his chest. "Let it all out."

She tilted her head. Her eyes were puffy and bloodshot from crying. "I don't need your pity."

He swiped the dampness from her cheeks and pressed his lips against her forehead. "That's not what this is." He cupped her face. "I feel your pain as deeply as I felt my mom's and Tina's. I watched my mother suffer in silence. You know how much the cruelty of her isolation affected me. I won't stand on the other side of that door and let you go through this alone."

"You don't understand." She bolted upright, clutching the covers to her chin. "A year after Rosy died, I knew I needed to leave Pete, yet I stayed. I knew better, but for some ridiculous reason, I thought he'd change. Or maybe I thought I could change him."

"Babe. Don't do this to yourself." He fluffed a pillow and leaned against the headboard, knowing she needed a little space. This wasn't his first rodeo. "My sister didn't leave her ex at first because she was afraid of what people would think and the fact that she, of all people, should *know better* because of our dad. Abusers never start out in a relationship with fists."

"Don't tell me shit I know." She tucked her hair behind her ears. "I don't need you to be conde-scending or to remind me of all the pitfalls of what happens to battered women. All I need is to cry it out."

"I'm not stopping you from doing that. But there's no point in being alone when there's someone who cares about you and is willing to hold you until you're done or fall asleep."

"Why do you care? I mean, you hated me for years."

He arched both brows. "What the hell are you talking about?" This was not a response he expected, nor was he sure how to deal with it. "I've never hated you."

"Come on. I cheated on you. Got pregnant. Married someone else, and then you didn't speak to me for fifteen years until I accidentally called you. And now you all of a sudden give a shit?"

He blew out a puff of air and raked a hand through his unruly hair, which desperately needed a cut.

Her ramble was deflection at its best and he contemplated if he should even give it life. However, they did have their own unresolved issues that he did want to discuss. He figured they'd do it after Pete was back behind bars and her divorce was more than just a filing. But hell, if she wanted to get her mind off the current problem, he'd go there—for her.

"First, you didn't cheat on me. We'd broken up."

"That's a technicality."

"Maybe so, but let's not forget that two months before that I was the one who stepped out on you."

He lowered his chin. "I don't know why you've always given me a pass on that."

She poked him dead center in the chest. "I was pissed as hell and hurt when you did that. But you told me and I forgave you. We did our best to get past it. And let's not forget, we were also broken up or on a break or whatever when it happened. Not to mention, she was some nameless, faceless girl you met at some party at school. Not someone we both knew. And she didn't end up pregnant."

Closing his eyes, he counted to ten.

"I hate it when you do that. It means you're contemplating saying something I won't like."

"I don't think this is the right time to rehash this." He blinked.

"Just say it."

"Fine." He folded his arms. "The only difference between the two situations outside of you having a child was that you married Pete." He pressed his finger over her mouth when she opened it. "After I told you I still loved you. That I didn't care about what happened and that I'd raise that baby with you. I would have done whatever it took to make us work. But you didn't believe me."

"You think Pete was ever going to let that

happen?" She fell back on the bed. "I thought about having an abortion, but it was too late."

He rolled to his side, running his finger up and down her arm. "I'm sorry that I abandoned you. I should have fought harder for us."

"I'm being an asshole," she mumbled. "I hurt so I want everyone around me to be in as much pain as I'm in."

"I get it."

"Sometimes I hate when you're this understanding. A part of me thinks I married Pete out of spite."

"I know I moved to Montana and cut off all communication with anyone associated with Whiskey Ranch out of anger and frustration. I thought if I spoke to anyone, I'd ask about you or want to see you, and I was always afraid of what I'd do to Pete."

"You can be jealous." She laughed. "Remember Henry McGraw?"

"He was hitting on my girl right in front of me. What did you expect me to do?"

"Not throw your beer in his face." She rested her cheek on her hands and smiled. "I'm just glad you didn't hit him."

"I thought about it."

"I know."

Being with her like this brought back so many good memories. He wanted to relish in every single one. "I'm not the only one who could be possessive. I recall one time when you threw horse manure at someone because you thought they were flirting with me."

"That bitch Susie was absolutely giving you google eyes. And she made fun of the fact she had big boobs and I was in a training bra. She used to tell me that if she flashed you her nice round tits, you'd drop me like a hot potato."

"That was never going to happen. But I got so much shit for having a twelve-year-old girlfriend when I was fourteen and a freshman in high school," he said. "You'd come watch practice with all the other girlfriends and my teammates would call me a cradle robber, among other things. It eased up eventually. Two years isn't a big age gap. But I had been in love with you since the fifth grade."

"I used to tell JD I was going to marry you when I was like three."

"He has pictures of you in a little wedding dress and cowboy boots."

She groaned. "That's so embarrassing."

"I think it's cute." He reached out and brushed some of her hair from her face. The bruising around her eyes had turned a deep black and purple. It hurt his heart. "Everyone thought we were the most disgusting couple."

"My dad thought you were a cornball, but he adored you."

"I miss your dad. He was a good man."

"I wish he were here," she whispered. "I wish I could remember my mom."

Austin hadn't meant to bring up a painful memory such as her father's death. He tugged her closer. "You're not alone."

"I know that, but sometimes it feels like I am. Not only did Pete isolate me from friends and family, but I've been so ashamed of what my life has become."

Leaning in, he brushed his lips over her mouth. A fire ignited deep in his gut. He cut the kiss short. This was not the time. They may never get the chance to rekindle their love and he had to be okay with that. His role right now was to offer her comfort, a shoulder to cry on, and to be a good friend. "I know you don't want to hear this, but you're still young. You have time to rebuild and start fresh. And you have an entire family of crazy people to love you."

She smiled. "Thank you for invading my personal space tonight."

"Anytime." He sat up.

"Austin?"

"Yes?" He glanced over his shoulder.

"Will you stay with me?"

"Of course, but can we go to my bed? It's bigger and more comfortable. As a matter of fact, I'm going to order a new mattress tomorrow. This one sucks."

"Thank God. I wasn't going to say anything, but it's killing my back."

He jumped to his feet and offered a hand. "Come on. I promise to stay on my side of the bed."

She burst out laughing.

"What's so funny?"

"You said those exact words to me the first night we had sex."

"The difference between that night and tonight is I had no intention of keeping that promise and I had a box full of condoms," he said. "What you need is a good night's sleep and maybe a nice long hot bath in the morning."

"That's sounds wonderful."

He tugged her down the hall and into his room. "I'm also being a little selfish."

"What do you mean?" She climbed into his bed, curling up on her side.

He turned out the light and joined her. "I won't be able to sleep if I'm worried that you're having another moment."

Playfully, she slapped his shoulder. "I can't tell if you're pulling my leg or not."

"I'm dead serious. I hate that you're in so much emotional pain and that I can't fix it." He cupped the back of her neck and kissed her tenderly. "I've never stopped thinking or caring about you. I know the timing is all fucked up and your situation is diffi-cult, but I want you to know I'm here for you. I'm not going anywhere and you can count on me."

"Please don't make me cry." She snuggled into his body. She was warm and soft and he didn't want to ever let her go again.

"I don't want to ever be the reason you shed a tear. However, I'm here to hold you if you need to let it out."

Her hot lips landed on the center of his chest. She sighed. "Good night, Austin."

"Sleep well," he managed.

5

The next couple of days flew by in a haze. Cinnamon spent her days at the educational center working at the front desk while she waited for the background check to come back and her nights were filled with dinners with her family. She enjoyed catching up with all her cousins, spouses, and kids.

By the time she returned to Austin's cabin, she was bone-tired.

Austin had returned to his role on the ranch, working with the horses. Watching how some people treated him because of the rumors about his ex-fiancée broke her heart. The fact anyone believed he could have killed her was beyond Cinnamon's comprehension. She understood

Austin had a temper and could be the jealous type. She'd seen it firsthand. But murder? Never.

Austin opened the door to Boone's Bar and Grill. "You're going to love this place. The owner is married to Paget."

"She's so sweet," Cinnamon said. "I can't believe how much has changed at the ranch, and yet so much is exactly the same."

"I felt the same way when I got back."

"Austin. So good to see you." Boone, the owner of the bar and Paget's husband, raced to greet them. "You must be Cinnamon. I've heard a lot about you from your cousins."

"I hope it's all been good." Reluctantly, Cinnamon removed her sunglasses. The swelling on her face had gone down and the bruises didn't look half as bad, but they were still noticeable.

"Irish might have told a funny story or two." Boone smiled.

"How's little Henry?" Austin asked.

Boone tapped his chest. "I didn't think I could love anyone as much as I love that little boy. Even when he's being a little stinker." Boone smiled. "Why don't you follow me to the back patio? I've got one of our best tables out there."

"Sounds perfect."

"I'll take care of you personally," Boone said. "Can I start you off with a drink?"

"I'll take a scotch on the rocks."

"And what about for the lady?" Boone snagged a couple of menus and headed toward the back of the restaurant.

"Can you make a Cinnamon Cider Whiskey Sour?" Cinnamon asked.

Austin burst out laughing.

Cinnamon elbowed him in the side. "Don't make fun of the drink or the name."

Boone chuckled. "My wife lives for a good whiskey sour, which always makes me laugh considering her maiden name is Sour."

"Try going through life with the name Cinnamon Cider Whiskey and actually enjoying the drink." Cinnamon first tried the beverage when she'd been seventeen, making her lips pucker. But the older she got, the more she liked it.

"You'll be happy to know that I make a mean one." Boone set the menus on one of the tables. "I'll bring those right out along with a teaser of some of our best appetizers."

"Thanks, Boone." Austin pulled out a chair for Cinnamon.

He'd always been such a gentleman and while

she never needed that kind of treatment, she always appreciated that about Austin.

"This place is nice. Thanks for taking me out tonight." Ever since she'd been back, after spending time with family, she always cried in Austin's arms half the night. She didn't know why the tears came every time she laid her head on the pillow. She was glad to be away from Pete. It was a relief to be starting over. But not knowing where Pete was had started to grate on her nerves. While she hadn't reached out to anyone she knew in Boise, Brad's contacts had told him that no one had seen him since he'd been bailed out. The closer it got to his first appearance in court, the more she felt on edge.

"I thought you might like getting out of the house for a change. And it is Friday night."

"I've honestly been afraid to leave the ranch."

"Why?" Austin asked.

"Afraid of what people are saying about me."

Austin nodded. "I get that." He glanced around. "To be honest, sometimes when I come into town, there are people who walk on the other side of the street when they see me."

She reached across the table and took his hand. "That's terrible. I would think that people would have realized you're innocent after a year."

"The problem is that about once a month either a federal agent comes to town or a story hits some news channel, stirring it all up again."

"Why don't you fight back? Make your own statement. Isn't that what Tom or whatever his name does?"

"That's what he used to do. Now when he speaks out, it's asking for help. He doesn't attack me anymore. And it's not that I haven't thought about it, but the one lawyer that JW had me talk to recommended that my silence is golden. That anything I say could end up being used against me in any courtroom or the court of public opinion if and when they do find Charity. Besides, at this point, I only care about what my friends and family think of me."

Boone returned with their drinks and tray of what smelled like a little piece of heaven. "The apps are on the house."

"You don't have to do that," Austin said.

"If I didn't, my wife would have my head, and you know that."

Austin smiled. "Thank her for me."

Boone nodded. "Do you know what you want?"

"I haven't had a chance to look at the menu," Cinnamon said. "Do you have a recommendation?"

"Of course, it's my restaurant." Boone tucked his long hair behind his ears. "You can't go wrong with the steak, burger, or pulled pork. But our Cobb salad is to die for if you want something lighter."

"Oh, I want the steak, medium rare. Does that come with a baked potato?" Cinnamon asked.

"I can make that happen. And our vegetable today is asparagus." Boone took her menu.

"Sounds great," she said.

"I'll have the same. Medium for me." Austin lifted his drink and sipped.

"He doesn't know how to eat meat." She shook her head. "He thinks if it's red and bloody, it's going to kill him."

"I just don't want it mooing at me." Austin laughed.

"I'll put your order right in." Boone turned but paused as the hostess brought a group of four to the patio.

One of the women pointed at Austin and whispered something to the hostess before turning and scurrying back inside.

Boone let out an exasperated sigh.

"I'm sorry," Austin said.

"Don't be." Boone tucked the menus under his arm. "I can't stand that woman anyway. If she never returned to this restaurant, it would be too soon."

"Why?" Cinnamon asked.

"Because she's a stuck-up bitch who likes to insert herself in other people's business," Boone said. "She actually had the nerve once to tell me that my son shouldn't be in my own place of business. I mean really. Paget and Henry stopped in right before the dinner rush one day and I was short-staffed, so I would have to stay that night. Kind of like tonight. Henry wanted to say good night to Daddy. No big deal. He was in and out. That freaking lady went off on me like I gave my kid a cigar and three fingers of scotch."

"She's coming back," Austin said.

"Since I seated you, the main dining room might have filled up with the exception of the few reserved tables. She might not have a choice." Boone cringed.

"I wish I had a cigar to light up and blow in her face," Cinnamon said.

"I have one in my office, but unfortunately even the patio is nonsmoking. Otherwise, I'd give you one." Boone leaned closer. "But if Paget knows I'm still sneaking them, she'll have my head."

"Your secret is safe with me." Cinnamon smiled.

Boone strolled back into the restaurant.

"He's adorable." Cinnamon winked.

"My jealous streak is coming out." Austin tilted his head.

"Come on, are you telling me you'd kick him out of bed?"

"I don't think anyone in their right mind would." Austin raised his glass. "To Boone."

She clanked her glass against his and then brought it to her lips. "Oh my God. We're taking him home."

"I don't think his wife would like that."

"She's cute. She can come too."

"I do have a thing for younger women."

Cinnamon kicked him under the table.

"Ouch." He winced. "You started it."

"And I'm finishing it." She plucked an onion ring from the plate. It had been months. No, years since she'd had this much fun. She only wished that Austin would stop glancing at the table where that woman had been seated.

Or that she could stop worrying about Pete.

She glanced over her shoulder.

The woman glared.

"What's your problem?" Cinnamon asked,

staring back, wondering where she'd gathered the courage to confront anyone about anything.

"Don't," Austin whispered. "It's not worth it."

The woman scoffed and lowered her gaze.

She'd lost her voice the day she married Pete. They'd go out in public and she'd never dare speak unless spoken to and only if Pete allowed it.

Never again would someone else tell her what to do or how to do it.

"No. I'm not going to sit here and let her judge you. Or me for that matter."

Austin arched a brow. "This coming from the woman who's been worried about what people think."

"Yeah, seeing how she just looked at you made me realize that I shouldn't care." She pushed back her chair.

Austin jumped to his feet. "Cinnamon. Please, don't cause a… do what you need to." To his credit, he sat back down.

She marched herself over to the woman's table. "Excuse me, ma'am. Do you have a problem with me or my date?"

"How dare you come over here and interrupt me and my family," the woman said. "And do you know who you're having dinner with?" The woman leaned closer. "Did he do that to your face?" she whispered.

Cinnamon gasped. "You have some nerve to make that assumption. While it's none of your business, no. He didn't. Actually, he's saving me from the man who did. My soon-to-be ex-husband. And for the record, that man over there is the kindest, sweetest, most gentle human being you could ever meet. You shouldn't go listening to gossip or rumors." She stared at the woman. "Oh my God. You're Mrs. Ledderman. Holy shit. Didn't your husband get arrested for fondling one of his students?"

Mrs. Ledderman's mouth dropped open like a brick. She cleared her throat. "I don't know what you're talking about. My name is Ms. Welch."

"Nope. I remember clear as day. I was in first grade. Your husband was the orchestra teacher at my friend's private school two towns over. You of all people should be kinder. I certainly wouldn't judge you by your ex-husband's actions. You shouldn't judge Austin or me, especially when he didn't do anything wrong. Now stop staring at us while we enjoy our fucking dinner." She turned on her heel and marched back to the table.

Austin covered his mouth.

"You find that amusing?"

"I didn't recognize her," Austin said. "You have one wicked memory."

"It hit me like a ton of bricks when I looked at her. I felt so sorry for what she went through. But not anymore. She can suck dick for all I care."

"Well, it looks like the Cinnamon that I remember is back." Austin chuckled. "You still have a mouth like a truck driver."

"I thought you always liked that about me."

"Never said I didn't." He raised his glass to his lips. "Listening to you in the stands when I was playing football was always amusing. One of the coaches took me aside once and told me he never heard a girl with a more colorful mouth before."

"I take that as a compliment."

A server came out and placed their food on the table.

"Not that I haven't appreciated all my cousins' hospitality or their cooking, but this is a real treat." She dug into her steak.

"It's nice to see you relax and have a good time."

"I have to admit I was worried about coming out, but I'm glad we did."

"Me too." He smiled. "Maybe after this we can

go grab some ice cream at that shop around the corner."

"I'd like that." She raised her glass. "But I'm having another one of these first."

"Uh-oh. Are you still a lightweight?"

She nodded. "I promise to keep it at two."

"Why not three?" He winked. "Last time you did that I got lucky."

"You're mixing up our nights." She waved her fork. "If I have three, you'll be holding up my hair while I make love to the porcelain god."

"We don't want that."

She held his gaze for a long moment. She could get used to this and she wasn't sure if it was fleeting or real. They had so much history filled with a ton of baggage, both together and separate. Not to mention there was still so much of his life she didn't know.

"You're looking at me like you want to ask me something." He stuffed his face with some steak.

"I do."

"Go ahead."

"How did you meet Charity?"

"That's a question I didn't expect." He wiped his lips with his napkin and leaned back.

"You don't have to talk about her if you don't want to."

"It's fine." He sipped his drink. "I was working at a ranch in Montana."

"That's where you went after you graduated from college?"

He nodded. "I'd been there for about twelve years when Charity and her girlfriends came to the ranch on a girls' trip. They did not fit in at all and I found it insanely amusing. They were truly a bunch of fish out of water. Charity and I hit it off, but she was a guest and I kept her at a safe distance. However, she kept coming at me and I figured she'd be gone in a few days. Only she came back a month later."

"Why?"

He lowered his chin. "I can be charming when I want to be."

Cinnamon rolled her eyes. "I guess I asked, so go on."

"For the next seven or eight months, she'd visit me every couple of weeks. I kept telling her that I didn't do relationships. She took that as a challenge. I didn't think much about it."

Cinnamon held up her hand. "Did you have any girlfriends after we broke up?"

"Not really. I mean I dated, but nothing that lasted more than a year."

"I don't know if that makes me sad or if I'm flattered as hell."

He chuckled. "The first few years it was because I hadn't gotten over you, but as time passed, I just got used to being alone. I decided I liked sleeping in the middle of the bed."

"I've noticed. And you steal the covers."

"Well, you snore."

"I do not," she said, pushing her empty plate aside. "Go on. I'm sitting on the edge of my seat."

"Charity kept asking me to come visit her in Boise. I would tell her absolutely not. I told her that I had no intention of ever returning to Idaho. But after about a year, I decided that I liked her and she'd been coming to me, so I owed her at least one visit. It turned into two and then three. Finally, she begged me to move. She even found me a job at a ranch. Although, she absolutely hated me working there and after I moved, that became a thing."

"How long did you live there?"

"A little over a year, but I only worked at the ranch for three months."

"What the hell did you do if you didn't work on a ranch?" Cinnamon finished her drink and rested her elbows on the table. This answer should be interesting.

"I sold cars." He cringed. "It was the worst fucking job on the planet."

"Holy fuck. I can't believe you did that."

He shrugged. "I thought I was in love with her. Anyway, when JW offered me the job at Whiskey Ranch, I told Charity how miserable I was, which she already knew, and I said it was her turn to move for me. I honestly believed she would tell me to fuck off and we'd be done."

"Were you engaged by this time?"

He nodded.

"You actually proposed to this woman?"

"No. She brought up marriage and then wanted to go shopping for a ring, but I always wanted my wife to wear my mother's ring."

"God, I hope she gave it back."

"She did." He let out a long breath. "Telling this story makes me feel a bit like a fool."

"Those are your words, not mine."

"Gee, thanks," Austin said.

"What did she know about me?"

"Everything and truth be told, she hated you, especially after you called, and then I became a bit obsessed with discovering more about what was going on with you."

"So, you thought moving her to my cousin's ranch would be a good idea." Cinnamon smacked her forehead. "I can't imagine that was easy for her."

"She hated every second of it, but I was happier than a pig in shit. But let's not forget, she was cheating on me, for months."

Cinnamon cocked her head.

"Let's not go down that road again. We've moved past all that when it comes to us," he said.

"Us. That's an odd thing to say."

"Why?"

"There is no us as in present. Only us as in the past," she said.

"You sleep in my bed every night." He lifted his drink and downed the last few drops. "You wake up in my arms every morning. That's something."

"I'm not divorced."

"I'm aware," he said. "But you will be."

"I'm going to have to testify in Pete's trial."

"You're not telling me anything I don't know." Austin reached across the table and took her hand. "I was half kidding about the sleeping arrangements. I understand why I'm holding you all night.

I don't pretend to believe there's anything but a lot of history between us. But are you going to tell me you don't have any feelings for me at all?"

"No," she admitted. "But it's too soon."

"I know. Part of me is just trying to make things light and keep you smiling. But you have to know that I've carried a piece of you around in my heart all these years and I can't just shut that off."

"I've done the same thing but for me, I can't simply turn it back on." She took his hand and squeezed. "The feelings are there. I care about you and am grateful for all you've done. But I need a little time before I jump into anything other than this friendship we've formed."

"I hear you loud and clear," he said. "Why don't we get the check, go get that ice cream, and then go home and watch a movie."

"That sounds like a great idea." A huge weight lifted from her shoulders. As much as she wanted to fall into his arms and make love to him again, it wasn't the right time. There was still so much confusion that swirled around in her mind. Too much unfinished business to deal with. However, when things with Pete settled, at least she knew there was hope for her and Austin and that made her soul sing.

Austin tossed the receipt with a nice tip on the table. He knew he didn't need to do that since the owner had waited on them. But Boone would do what he always did and share that tip with his staff. Austin glanced up and his face immediately tensed. His blood turned to fire. He stood, knocking over the chair.

"What's going on?" Cinnamon asked, glancing over her shoulder.

"Get behind me, now," Austin said behind a tight jaw.

Thankfully, she did exactly what he asked without hesitation.

"Mrs. Ledderman. Could you please get Boone and tell him to call Brad Logan at the sheriff's department?"

"It's Ms. Welch," she said with a testy tone.

"Sorry. Ms. Welch." Austin held up his arm, protecting Cinnamon. "Have Boone tell Sheriff Logan that I need assistance with Miss Whiskey's husband."

"That's who did that to her face?" Ms. Welch stood.

"Please. Just do it," Austin whispered.

Ms. Welch snagged one of the gentleman's hands that she came in with and scurried around a couple of tables and right past Pete, who was inching closer.

"Stay behind me, unless I tell you otherwise," Austin said. "And if something happens, I'm apologizing ahead of time."

"Step away from my wife." Pete stood eight feet away.

Everyone on the patio went silent.

"That's not going to happen," Austin said. "You're not welcome here, so if I were you, I'd leave."

"Not without my wife." Pete inched closer.

Cinnamon gripped Austin's shoulders, digging her nails into his skin. He could feel her body shake with the intensity of an earthquake.

He hated that Pete frightened her, taking away all her power. Men like him didn't deserve shit.

"She's not going anywhere with you. Ever. Now leave before I do something I'll regret."

"Are you threatening me? Please tell me you're threatening me so I can defend myself."

"Nope," Austin said. "I'm stating a fact." He had no idea if Brad was at home, on patrol, or at the station. Depending on where he was, it could take him five to fifteen minutes to get to Boone's Bar and Grill. If he was too far out, he'd send one of his men. Either way, Austin needed to buy some time. The last thing he wanted to do was toss a few punches around.

But he wasn't opposed to giving Pete a couple of black eyes.

However, he knew Cinnamon wouldn't approve and he didn't want to cause a bigger scene in his friend's restaurant.

Pete took two more steps closer.

Austin inched back. "Seriously, Pete. She doesn't want to go with you and I don't want any trouble."

"Trouble has a way of finding you wherever you go." Pete smiled. "And let my wife tell me she doesn't want to come home with me."

Cinnamon stepped to Austin's side. "I will never go anywhere with you again." She inched back behind Austin.

Thank God.

"You don't mean that," Pete said. "Now come on, honey. I've let you have your little temper tantrum. It's time to come home and put an end to this mess you've created for me." He stepped closer, reaching his arm out.

Austin puffed out his chest. "Back off. Besides,

you weren't supposed to leave Idaho Falls. The cops find you here, they will arrest you."

"No, they won't because my little wife back there will make sure all these stupid little charges are dropped." Pete narrowed his eyes. "Isn't that right, sweetie?"

"Like hell I am. You've bashed in my face for the last time," Cinnamon said with a shaky voice.

At least she had one now.

"I'm done playing games, Cinny." Pete's nostrils flared.

"Don't call me that. I hate it." Cinnamon wrapped her arms around Austin's middle, pressing her head to his back. "I'm staying right here."

"With him?" Pete made a *tsk tsk* noise. "You think I'm going to stand here and take this? You think I will let my wife be brainwashed and manipulated by this man? That's not going to happen. Not anymore. Let's go, Cinnamon."

Boone stepped out into the patio. "Excuse me. Is there a problem here?"

Pete turned. "Yeah. I'm trying to collect my wife and leave, but this asshole is holding her hostage."

"I doubt that," Boone said. "I don't believe the young lady wishes to go with you, sir. So, I'm going to have to ask you to leave. You're disturbing my patrons."

"I'll be happy to." Pete smiled. "With my wife."

Austin glared at Boone. While he wanted Pete gone, he much preferred it to be in handcuffs.

"Well, it appears she's not leaving with you, so please, don't make me physically remove you or call the police." Boone shifted his eyes.

Austin glanced in the same direction.

A cop car was parked outside on the side street.

Well, all right then. Austin would roll with it.

"I'm giving you one minute." Boone raised his cell. "Leave on your own accord or the police will be here in five. Your call."

"This isn't over." Pete turned.

Boone stopped him. "I'd prefer you go out the back. You've made my customers nervous."

"Fine," Pete said.

Austin stepped to the side, making sure Cinnamon stayed directly behind him.

Pete hissed as he passed. "I'll make sure you both pay for this," he whispered.

"Stay with Boone." Austin kissed her temple before following Pete out the back door where Brad and one of his deputies met him.

"What the fuck?" Pete stopped dead in his

tracks. He turned, but Austin was there to prevent him from returning to the patio.

"Pete Thompson," Brad said. "You're under arrest for harassment, breaking a restraining order, and failure to remain in Idaho Falls."

"This is bullshit," Pete protested. "You can't arrest me. I did nothing wrong."

"We'll be taking you back to Idaho Falls where you could end up remaining in lockup until your trial." Brad slapped the cuffs onto Pete. "You shouldn't have left Idaho Falls and you sure as shit shouldn't have sent harassing texts to your wife. Those will be given to the prosecutor handling your case. Deputy Markus, read this guy his rights." Brad strolled toward Austin. "I'm so glad you didn't hit him."

Austin wiggled his fingers. "I wanted to."

"I'm sure you did." Brad curled his fingers around Austin's biceps. "How's Cinnamon?"

"Shaken, but okay."

"Well, you better get back to her. I'll be in touch when he's back in Idaho Falls."

"Thank you."

"Anytime." Brad nodded.

Austin strolled back into the restaurant. No sooner did he step foot on the patio than

Cinnamon flung her arms around him and hugged him tight.

"I was so scared," she said.

"It's all right." He held her close. "He can't hurt you now."

She tilted her head, staring into his eyes with her big blue orbs. Tears dribbled down her cheeks. "No. I was afraid you were going to deck him and you'd end up in jail."

He chuckled. "I will admit that the thought did cross my mind." He brushed his lips across her mouth. "But I know you would have been mad if I had, so I chose not to."

"Can we skip the ice cream and just go home?"

"Your wish is my command." He laced his fingers through her hand and tugged. "Boone, I'm so sorry about all that."

"Hey, no worries. I'm just glad Brad got here in time before anything bad happened and they were actually able to arrest him."

"You and me both." Austin nodded.

"Excuse me," Ms. Welch said. "I wanted to apologize for my behavior. I shouldn't have been so quick to judge based on rumors. What you just did for this young woman took courage. I can see she's been through a lot."

"Everyone has a story, Ms. Welch," Austin said. "Don't think twice about it and thank you for going to get Boone. It is greatly appreciated."

"You're a kind man." She glanced over her shoulder. "I would have hit the bastard."

He smiled. "You have a lovely night."

"You as well." For the first time in a long while, Austin felt as though he not only could hold his head high, but that he had a future and it was looking pretty bright for a change.

6

Cinnamon splashed cold water on her face and stared at herself in the bathroom mirror. She looked like a raccoon. Or something straight from a horror movie. She lifted her shirt over her head. Her side didn't hurt half as much. Neither did her thigh. The doctor said the stitches could come out in five days. She'd passed that.

She shimmied out of her jeans and ran her hand over the wound on her leg. Flashes of Pete coming at her with a knife filled her brain. She'd never been so scared in her life. She honestly thought she was going to die and all because she had used the computer.

She pressed her hands against the vanity. She needed to tell Austin the truth about what happened. Why Pete lost his shit so bad that night and a few other things. She also wanted these stitches out. They itched like hell.

Sucking in a deep breath, she opened the bathroom door and entered the master bedroom.

Austin was sprawled out in the bed with his back propped up on pillows and a book in his hands. He glanced up and his eyes went wide. He cleared his throat and lowered his novel to his lap. "Are you aware you're not wearing anything but a bra and a thong?"

"I want you to take these stitches out." She sat on the edge of the bed.

"Excuse me?" He blinked.

"I've seen you do it on horses and other animals before."

"But I've never done it on a human." He set his book on the nightstand.

"It can't be that much different."

He ran his hand across her midsection, fingering one set of stitches and then the other before moving to the set on her leg. "I suppose your wounds look as though they are entirely closed."

"They're driving me crazy. Please, take them out."

"All right. Let me see if I've got something small

enough. What I use on horses will be too big." He pulled back the covers. "But could you at least put on some shorts? There are boxers in the top drawer of my dresser. I've been able to keep my hands to myself while you're sleeping in my bed, but that thong is going to change things real quick."

She laughed. "I thought you liked this style."

"That's the problem and there's only so much a man can take. I'm going to need a cold shower now before I go to bed." He made his way to the bathroom.

While he rummaged through the medicine cabinet, she found a pair of his boxers and hiked them up to her hips. They were a little too big, so she rolled the elastic down, hoping that would help hold them up. At least for a little while. She hoped that after she told him the truth, he wouldn't be too mad—at least he shouldn't be. If anything, he should be flattered.

And then maybe they could deal with what was obviously happening between them. Her feelings were real. She knew that deep in her soul. They had never died and she wanted to explore them. It didn't matter that she'd just left her husband because that marriage had died the day they buried their daughter.

Maybe even before.

Her heart had always belonged to Austin and Pete knew it. That fact had made him go crazy.

"Okay." Austin strolled into the bedroom carrying a small pair of scissors and some ointment. "This should do the trick."

"You don't sound very confident."

"Hey, you're the one who asked me to do this, so lie down and let me work." He pressed his hand on the center of her chest and gave her a playful shove. Pinching her stomach, he tugged at the stitches and began removing them one by one. "Let me know if I'm hurting you."

"It feels so good to get those things out of my body. I just want to scratch like mad."

"Don't do that. I'll put this cream on when I'm done. That should help. It will also help with scarring, so use it a couple of times a day."

"I'm not worried about the battle wounds. They are reminders of what I escaped." She lifted her head and glanced down.

He'd removed one set and was rubbing the warm cream on her stomach. "I'm so sorry about what you had to endure. I'm also sorry that I scared you tonight. But you should have been more frightened of him."

"Trust me, he terrifies me. But I didn't want you to get into a fight and land yourself in county lockup. I know you, and you don't hold back when your buttons are pushed. I also know Brad and he wouldn't hesitate to slap cuffs on you, especially if it was for your own good. But that would have left me alone and that scares me more."

"I'm here for you." Austin moved to the next set of stitches. "I've grown up a little in the last fifteen years. I have more restraint."

"Perhaps, but your rage was palpable."

He leaned over and kissed her scar. "Can you blame me? Look at what that asshole did to you." He pinched her thigh and tugged at the stitch with his fingers before making the first snip.

"Tonight could have been really bad for you."

"Me?" Austin jerked his head. "What about you? All that man was focused on was getting his hands on you."

"That's only part of what he wanted."

"What do you mean?" Austin finished rubbing the ointment on her leg. He stood and pulled out a shirt from his dresser and handed it to her. Climbing onto the bed, he fluffed a pillow and eased in next to her.

She sat up and let out a long breath. "I didn't

accidentally call you that night I said I meant to call JW."

"Then why did you say that?"

"I'd managed to lock Pete in the bedroom after he beat the shit out of me. I called the cops, and then I called you."

Austin closed his eyes. "Why did you hang up on me?"

"Because Pete managed to get out."

"What happened when the cops got there?" He blinked, taking her hand and kissing the back of it.

"I told them it was a mistake and that I fell down the stairs. They tried to separate us so they could talk to me alone, which they did. But I kept to my story because if I didn't, I was afraid he'd go crazy and kill me because of you."

"He knew you called me?"

"Pete had found a journal I had been writing in, which had many references to you, about how I missed you and made a mistake in marrying Pete."

"Jesus," Austin muttered. "All your texts now make sense."

"In my phone I had you listed as Audrey. I don't know when he figured out Audrey was you, but he did."

"Did this have anything to do with me?" He waved his hand over her body.

Tears stung the corners of her eyes. "This isn't your fault."

"I know that. But I still want to know what happened."

"You stopped texting and for some reason that crushed me. It had been years since we talked and getting those random texts brightened my day. When they stopped, I felt more alone than I had in years. I risked journaling again. He found them, as usual."

"What kinds of things did you write?"

"How I missed Whiskey Ranch. My cousins. You." She swiped at her cheeks. "He had taken my phone and shut off the internet when he was out of the house. I wasn't allowed to work and my only friends were the ones he approved of, which were like none. I would sneak down early in the morning while he was in the shower to use the computer and google you."

"You did what?" He jerked his head.

"I know that sounds crazy."

"No." He took her chin with his thumb and forefinger. "It's sweet." He brushed his lips across hers in a tender, romantic kiss. His tongue darted into her mouth.

She gripped his shoulders. Her muscles filled with heat.

"Continue," he whispered.

"I was reading about what happened with Charity when I realized Pete was standing right behind me. I have no idea how long he'd been there. But I had googled your name and other things about you, so when he checked the search history, at least a dozen items had Austin Sawyer in it. But what was worse, he had my journal in his hands and that's when he went nuts. He slammed my head into—"

"I don't want the details of the beating." Austin ran his thumb across her cheek. "I can see what he did to you and that's enough."

"For fifteen years Pete has been insanely jealous of you. There were times he'd asked me if Rosy was yours because she had blue eyes while his were brown."

"You have blue eyes."

"I know and Rosy couldn't be yours because of the timing. Besides, I did a paternity test to prove it to him because I was so tired of listening to it." She pressed her hand on Austin's chest. "This was before he started beating me. While he was always possessive, it took a while for things to get this bad."

"Don't make excuses for him."

"I'm not. I'm telling you what it was like. My marriage was never good. In the beginning Pete used to say there were three of us in our bed and the reality is that sometimes he was right. I never got over you. I tried. I focused on Rosy and believe it or not, Pete was a good dad."

"How can you say that if he questioned if he was even her father?"

"He did that to hurt me. He never treated her badly. Only me. When she was diagnosed with cancer, he was at her bedside the entire time. He was attentive to her but blamed me for her getting sick. He would say that if I wasn't thinking about you all the time, it wouldn't have happened."

Austin pinched the bridge of his nose. "I understand how hard it is to leave an abusive relationship, so this question is hard to ask. But why didn't you leave him back then? Why didn't you contact me if you still wanted to be with me?"

"Do you remember exactly what you said to me after you offered to raise my baby with me?"

"You mean after you told me to go to hell? Yeah. I remember. I told you that if you went through with the marriage never to contact me again and to enjoy your life."

"It was a little harsher than that. But I took it to heart and did my best to make things work with Pete. When Rosy died, I was devastated."

Austin took her hand and squeezed.

"I went into a deep depression and so did Pete. He was drinking heavily and I could barely get out of bed. All I wanted was to come back to Whiskey Ranch. To see my family. To call you. I tried to find you. I reached out to all my cousins, but no one knew where you were. When Pete found out I had been looking for you, that's when the isolation really began and because I was in such a bad headspace, I didn't even see it happening."

"You can't blame yourself for that."

"Again, I'm not doing that. But there was a part of me that felt as though I deserved to be punished. I know that's not true. However, you have to under-stand that when I realized what a huge mistake I had made, in my young mind, I believed that I somehow brought on all the misery. A few years went by. I sought counseling, first with Pete's bless-ing, but when I started to get better and gain confi-dence, he took that away from me. Eventually, I became numb to it all until I couldn't take it anymore. But even then, I couldn't commit to leaving for a couple of years. He threatened to hurt my family. To destroy you. He told me he knew where you were and that he'd make sure you'd suffer."

"How did you get my phone number? Because I changed it. And you never changed yours, which I find odd because I would think Pete would have wanted you to."

"He allowed it to keep my family from freaking out, but he controlled the communication and it's not that hard to find cell numbers these days. Besides, I asked Irish for it once I knew you were back at the ranch."

"Irish never told me that."

"Because I begged him not to."

"That man does know how to keep a secret," Austin said. "All this time, I thought you wanted nothing to do with me."

"I'm sorry I hurt you. I was young and made many mistakes, but I can't say Rosy was one of them."

He kissed her nose. "I'm so sorry about her passing. It breaks my heart that you had to go through that. I wish I could have met her."

"She was a sweet little girl."

"I'm sure she was." Austin pulled her close. "I don't know if this is bad timing or not, but I feel compelled to tell you that I've spent the last fifteen years thinking about you too. Every woman I've ever dated was never good enough because they weren't you. I can't tell you how many times some chick broke up with me because I was still hung up on you. The only one who didn't was Charity, but she was cheating on me anyway." He laughed. "Funny thing though, the second she walked onto this ranch, she bitched about all the things here that were all about Cinnamon, including the box I have under this bed." He leaned over and pulled it out. "This has all the stupid little notes you used to pass me in the hallways at school. Some of the cards you sent me in college. Pictures. All sorts of sappy sentimental stuff. I had to hide it so she wouldn't burn it."

"Shit, Pete did burn mine."

"Now I wish I had hit him," Austin said.

Cinnamon lifted the lid off the box and pulled out one of the notes. "I can't believe you kept all this stuff. You were always sentimental and little sappy, but I would have never expected this."

"I'll be honest, there were a couple of times I thought about getting rid of them." He held an old birthday card in his hands. "But every time I tried, it felt like I was tossing away a piece of my heart."

She continued to thumb through some pictures. "Oh my God. This was from my freshman formal. You look so handsome in that suit."

"I hated it."

"I know. You bitched about it half the night."

"We did make a good-looking couple though." He took the image from her hands, stuffed it in the box, and set it aside. "Is it crazy that I still care about you?" He palmed her cheek. "Dare I say, even love you."

She swallowed her beating heart. "I don't think I've ever stopped loving you," she said. "I worry, though, that all my feelings are past memories. I don't know the man you are today and you don't really know me anymore."

"That's easily remedied." He ran his hand through her long hair. "Whiskey Ranch is your home. I'm certainly not going anywhere. There's no reason why we can't start fresh."

"That sounds so cliche."

"Don't you believe it's possible?"

She leaned in and kissed his sweet lips, letting them linger for a long, delectable moment. It truly was like she'd returned to the very place she'd always belonged. "We've hurt each other in ways many could never come back from."

"And yet we're in each other's arms right now." He arched a brow. "Outside of running into Pete, I had a great time tonight. I don't think I've felt this alive in years and that's all because of you."

"I know what you mean, but I don't want to rush things because of our history, which is a total switch from when I walked out of that bathroom, because I had every intention of trying to seduce you."

He chuckled. "I wasn't born yesterday. I figured that out when you weren't wearing much. But I take it you've changed your mind."

"It's not that. I still want you. I'm just wondering if maybe it might be better if we wait."

"Like until morning?"

She slapped his shoulder.

"Okay, tomorrow night?"

"You're impossible."

"I'm kidding," he said. "I never thought I'd ever have a second chance with you, so if waiting a week, two, or a month is what you need, I can do that."

"Oh my God. This reminds me of the first time you tried to have sex with me. You were so patient."

"Only you didn't make me wait for more than three days." He held up three fingers and waggled his brows. "You texted me after football practice and asked me to meet you at your place. I didn't know your dad was gone for the night."

"The look on your face was classic when I met you at the door in a tiny nighty, holding a box of condoms."

"You were sixteen. Way too young to be having sex." He smacked his head. "What was I thinking?"

"You were a horny teenager who hadn't had sex yet yourself."

"This is true and imagine my surprise when my girlfriend turned out to be a sex addict."

"I was not." She scowled. "I just liked sex with you."

"I had no idea what I was doing."

"You could have fooled me." She yawned. "Is it okay if I still stay in here with you tonight? If it's too—"

He pressed his finger over her lips. "I'll sleep better with you at my side, especially until I get word that Pete is tucked back into a jail cell in Idaho Falls."

"What happens if they let him out again?"

"Babe, we'll deal with it if they do, but trust me

when I say, I'll do whatever it takes to make sure you're safe." He pulled back the covers and pulled them over their bodies. "Get some sleep. Tomorrow we can take a nice leisurely horseback ride and have a picnic."

"That sounds like a little piece of Whiskey Ranch heaven." She rolled to her side, tucking her back against his chest, and closed her eyes. For the first time since she arrived home, the tears didn't come.

7

The weekend flew by in a haze of happiness. Cinnamon couldn't remember the last time she'd felt this free and light. Austin hadn't left her side for two days. He'd taken her horseback riding. He'd cooked her dinner and served her breakfast in bed. They spent Sunday with the rest of the family at JD and Annette's house. It felt good to be home.

While she continued sleeping in Austin's bed, he didn't push sex. He respected her wishes in wanting to take things slow. They had a few make-out sessions and she wanted to cave sometimes, but she had other concerns about making love.

Like the fact she hadn't liked it anymore. Sex with Pete hadn't been enjoyable the last few times they had it and if Austin knew there had been occasions when it wasn't consensual, he'd go ballistic.

Another truth she needed to tell him, but that would have to wait for another day.

There was still so much that hung over her head.

Pete might still be in jail, but he had a hearing to determine if the judge would make him stay there until his trial. That thought terrified her because she did not doubt that he'd return to Whiskey Ranch if given his freedom.

"Hey, babe. Is there any more coffee left?" Austin strolled from the master bedroom into the kitchen, smelling of fresh pine. His hair was damp from his shower and his face was free of stubble. He wore a pair of faded jeans and a black T-shirt. He set his Stetson on the counter.

"I already put some in your travel mug." She handed it to him. "There are a few strips of bacon left too."

"Mmm. Yum." He kissed her cheek.

A knock at the door startled her and she jumped. "Sorry. I'm so nervous about today."

"You tossed and turned half the night. I know you're worried, but the DA's office said they'd call us as soon as anything has been decided." He patted her bottom as he moved toward the front of the house.

"I know. I know." She pulled out one of the stools in front of the counter and plopped her ass on it. Lifting her mug, she sipped her coffee.

"Luke. Georgia Moon. What brings the two of you out here this morning?" Austin said.

"I need your help with an injured bull," Luke said. "He got tangled up in some barbed wire and the vet's not around for a couple of hours."

"Bulls are not what I'm known for, but I'm happy to go take a look," Austin said. "Why don't we call Gage to give me a hand. He's always been good at assisting me with stuff like this."

"Gage asked for some time off. Something about wanting to go visit relatives," Georgia Moon said. "I thought it strange because he's never once asked for vacation time."

"Not to mention he hasn't talked to his siblings since the fire that took his family," Luke said. "He hasn't spoken to them in years."

"Maybe this is a good thing," Austin said.

"I don't know about that." Cinnamon had spent many hours listening to Gage discuss how his siblings blamed him and refused to attend the funeral. "He told me it would be a cold day in hell before he ever forgave them. What exactly did he say?"

"He sent us a text message," Georgia Moon said. "All it said was that he was going to see his family and that he needed a week or so to deal with some personal things. We told him not to worry and take as long as he needed. That if we could do anything for him, not to hesitate to reach out. He's always been such a loyal employee that we felt it was the least we could do."

"That doesn't sound like Gage," Austin said. "However, he is getting older and I can see how he might want to reconcile with his siblings." He nodded. "We should get going. I don't want that bull to suffer."

"Me neither," Luke said.

"I'm going to stay here and visit with Cinnamon for a bit." Georgia Moon scurried into the kitchen. "I hear you're going to start working in the infant room today."

"I am." Cinnamon smiled. "I'm so excited."

"Did you fill out the application for school yet?" Austin snagged his Stetson.

Cinnamon shook her head.

Austin scowled. "The deadline is approaching."

He waggled his finger. "Don't start with me about the money. It will get figured out."

She rolled her eyes.

"I'll see you tonight." Austin leaned in and kissed her a little too hard on the lips in front of her cousin and Luke. "Have a great day with the babies." He followed Luke out the door with a spring in his step.

"He's happy this morning." Georgia Moon pulled down a mug and poured some coffee before sitting on a stool. "Something you want to share?"

"Nothing's happened." Cinnamon was close to all her cousins, but she and Georgia Moon had a unique friendship. It had been strained because of Pete, and they hadn't talked for many years. But as kids, they were close and Cinnamon was glad to have that friendship back. "I'm not ready yet."

"Why not? It's obvious to everyone how much the two of you still love each other."

"That's not the problem." Cinnamon groaned, dropping her head to the counter. "There's one thing I haven't told him yet and I don't know how he's going to take it. Not to mention, I don't know how I'll react to a sexual encounter."

Georgia Moon ran her hand up and down Cinnamon's back. "I'm sure Austin's brain has already gone there, because the rest of us have already thought it or talked about it."

Cinnamon jerked upright. "What the hell?"

"Come on. You still have bruises on your face. Pete abused you. It goes without saying he most likely raped you too."

"How can you say that so flippantly?"

"I'm not." Georgia Moon held her gaze with a softness emanating from her tender eyes. "Are you going to tell me it didn't happen?"

"No." Cinnamon sighed. Her first thought had been to explain it away like she'd always done. She could come up with a million reasons why Pete had done the things he had, but she was done making excuses for that asshole. What happened was wrong. Criminal even. And if she were smart, she'd add it to the list of things she needed to testify against him for. "I feel such shame over what happened and every time I think I'm ready, I tense over the idea. I worry that I'll freak out. Or do what I did with Pete and leave my body and lie there like I'm dead."

"I'm not a psychiatrist, so I could be speaking out of my ass, but you've loved Austin since you were a kid. He's not Pete. He's a kind, sweet, gentle man who would walk on water for you. I'm sure things with him would be so different, especially if he knew your fears."

"You don't know him the way I do." Cinnamon shifted, straddling the stool. "He has a wicked jealous streak when it comes to me. He despises Pete more than ever for what he's done. I know it took a great deal of restraint on his part that night at Boone's place not to haul off and put a fist through Pete's nose."

"But he didn't because Austin has learned over the years that punching someone doesn't correct the wrong. It doesn't even make him feel all that better."

"And you know this how? He left Whiskey Ranch and had no contact with any of you for over a decade."

"Because I've seen it in action," Georgia Moon said. "A few months ago, we had an employee whose husband abused her and Austin tossed his ass off this ranch, but he didn't hit him. Just literally lifted him over his shoulder, tossed him in his truck, and drove him to the bus station where he handed him a ticket and warned him that if he ever saw him near Tamara or this ranch, all bets were off."

"Has that man ever returned?"

Georgia Moon shook her head. "Of course, my

husband went with Austin and carried a shotgun, which helped."

"Oh, Luke. God, I love that man. I'm so glad the two of you found each other."

"It was a long hard road, but I couldn't be happier." Georgia Moon squeezed Cinnamon's biceps. "You can be this happy too. With Austin. The two of you are meant to be together. This is your second chance."

"I'm scared. When I left him at nineteen, I was so angry at him for the roller-coaster ride he'd put me on the last year of our relationship. I was mad at myself for turning to Pete and getting pregnant. But at the same time, I was excited to be a mom. I wanted that baby so badly. My own little person to love. I pinned all my hopes on her and I failed her too." Once again, the tears came hot and fast.

"Oh, honey. No, you didn't. I understand that everything that is happening is bringing up so much pain and making you question the decisions you made. But what matters is what brought you to this moment in your life. You're going to be free of Pete and there is no reason why you can't start building a life here again. You've got job opportunities. You can go back to school and have the career you've always wanted. And you can have the man you love. You just have to tell yourself that you deserve it."

"Austin thinks I should see a therapist."

"What do you think?"

"I know he's right. I went to one for a brief time when Rosy died, but Pete was so against it." Cinnamon swiped at her cheeks. She reached for her coffee and sipped. "Austin looked up a few this morning and left them with me. He even offered to go with me if I thought it would help. Or at the very least, he said he'd sit in the waiting room while I did my thing. He's super supportive about everything and while I know he means it, I sometimes don't trust it."

"Because of Pete."

"Yeah. But also because of what happened after Austin's dad died. He went through a dark time."

"I remember. He blamed himself for a lot of things."

"He does that with me. As if he could have prevented what happened with Pete. He's constantly telling me he should have fought harder for us. We both have regrets. The thing is, I can never regret Rosy."

"I take it you've told him that."

Cinnamon nodded.

"And what does he say?"

"That he doesn't expect me to. That what's done is done. That we can't change the past. We can only move forward."

"I'm not sure I understand what the problem is then." Georgia Moon lowered her chin. "What are you so afraid of?"

"I don't know. Maybe being happy. I've forgotten what that looks like."

Georgia Moon smiled. "There's only one way to find out and that's to let it happen." She kissed Cinnamon's cheek. "I need to get back to the bull riding school and you need to get to your first official day at the nursery. Trust me. Let Austin in. It's going to be worth the risk and you know your heart and soul want it."

"You're right." Cinnamon rose and squared her shoulders. "I'll send in the application for college today. Call a therapist. And I'll tell Austin the truth tonight."

"Good for you and call me anytime you want to talk. I'm always here for you."

"Thanks. I really appreciate how you and everyone else have welcomed me back."

"Are you kidding? You're family. We've missed you." Georgia Moon looped her arm around Cinnamon's waist. "This place hasn't been the same without you."

8

Austin pushed open the door to the cabin. "Cinnamon? Are you home?"

"In the kitchen."

He tossed his Stetson on the sofa and kicked off his boots. "Are you cooking? It smells like… I don't know… is that pasta or something?"

"Fettuccine Alfredo. At least it's what I'm trying to make. I have no idea if it will be any good or not. I've never been the best cook."

"I'm sure it will be great." He took the beer she offered and leaned against the counter.

She'd pulled her hair into some bun thing on the top of her head. She wore jeans, a white tank top, with an apron, and bare feet. The sexiest thing he'd ever seen. "Did you have a good day with the babies?"

"It was the best. I can't wait to go back tomorrow. Oh, and you'll be happy to know that I sent in my college application today. But…" She waved a spatula in his face.

He leaned back and arched a brow.

"…it's incomplete because of the financial aspect. I'm still married to dickface so I can't apply for financial aid."

"I told you that I'd pay for it."

"I don't want your money."

"Then you can pay me back when you get your divorce and go from there," he said. "Consider it a loan."

"You have an answer for everything."

"I'm a smart man."

She set the spatula on the counter and shoved two plates in his gut. "You're a wiseass is what you are and while I appreciate the gesture, I need to be on my own two feet."

"Babe. Right now, you have no credit cards, no money, and everything is wrapped up with your soon-to-be ex." He set his beer on the counter, moved to the other side of the kitchen, and did as he was told. Not just because she asked, but he knew her well enough that getting out of her way while he had this conversation was for his own safety. "I understand you want to do this on your own terms. I respect that. But Pete is in jail. Even if this case doesn't go to trial and he plea-bargains it out, we both know he will fight you in this divorce."

"Not to mention he won't give me a dime."

"All the more reason to let me give you a loan." He made sure he chose the words she would want to hear, even if that meant he'd have to let her pay him back. He didn't want that because eventually he wanted a life with her, and to him, that meant they shared everything fifty-fifty. But until they reached that point, he'd agree with her borrowing the money.

"I could get a loan from a bank."

"Interest rates are high and don't shoot the messenger, but you haven't had a job long enough for a bank to take that risk. I, on the other hand, wouldn't charge you interest and I know you're good for it."

"You're going to argue with me until I say yes, aren't you?" She carried a large plate of pasta and set it on the table. She smoothed down the front of her apron and sighed.

"I'm not arguing. I'm pointing out facts. And hopefully being a good boyfriend."

"Oh, is that what you think you are?"

"I'm not?" He raced to the other side of the counter, grabbed his beer, and chugged.

"You are." She laughed, although it was a nervous one. "But you might not be after this dinner."

"Why? Are you really expecting that it will taste that bad?"

"No." She turned and lifted a bottle of wine and poured a glass. "But the dinner conversation is going to be tough."

"Uh-oh. Let me fill my belly first." He sat down and stuffed his face with a big forkful. "Holy shit. This is actually really good."

"I'm glad you like it." She let out a long breath. "I need to tell you something and it's going to upset you."

He wiped his mouth with his napkin and leaned back. "I'm listening."

"It's about Pete."

"He will be in jail until his hearing and hopefully, the judge will keep him there." His appetite disappeared. He had a good idea where this conversation was headed. He had suspicions about some of the underlying issues Cinnamon had been having regarding intimacy. He didn't need to be a counselor or a doctor to figure that one out. He'd opted not to pry or pressure her into talking about it, much less doing anything other than snuggling or kissing. When she was ready, they'd deal with it.

He had his own set of problems that he would have to share, which would also have to be tonight, making this evening even harder. The only reason he knew anything about what was going on with the investigation into Charity's disappearance was that his brother-in-law had heard about it through his buddy at the FBI.

"I know and I feel better knowing he's there. I just wish he'd sign the divorce papers. I called the lawyer today and nothing has been done regarding that. I don't want it to go on forever."

"It won't. Eventually, whether it be because he signs them or because it goes before a judge, it will happen."

She twirled her pasta around her fork, but never brought it to her mouth. She stared at her food as if it were going to speak for her, so Austin decided to make it easier.

He reached across the table and took her hand. "Cinnamon, look at me."

She lifted her gaze.

"I shouldn't assume anything about what happened in your marriage, but a lot has gone on inside my head. Since you've been home, I've had nightmares about it."

"What do you mean?"

He touched the side of her face. "Your bruises are disappearing. The scars are healing, but I know there is more to this story you haven't told me. I haven't asked because I know it's painful. Shameful. Embarrassing and a whole list of other emotions for you. However, you need to know that I don't see you as the sum of what he did to you. I'm angry as hell. I hate knowing he hurt you emotionally, physically, sexually. I blame myself for it, even though I know there was nothing I could have done. I hope that asshole rots in prison for the rest of his life. But what he did has nothing to do with you or how I feel about you. It doesn't change the fact that I love you."

Tears fell from her eyes. "Why do you have to be so kind and know all the right things to say and at precisely the perfect moment?"

He pulled her from her chair to his lap. Wrapping his arms around her, he kissed her neck. "I don't know. I know you were struggling to tell me something, and I took a stab in the dark at what it could be based on how you pull away."

"I don't want to be like this."

"Babe, I know that. And you won't be forever. Did you call any of those therapists and schedule an appointment?"

"I have one on Friday."

"Would you like me to come?"

She cupped his face. "You have to work."

"Come on. You know how this ranch operates. It will be okay if I let JW know I need to sneak off for a few hours for something."

"All right. I'd like that."

"Good. Now, I have something I need to discuss with you," he said.

"That sounds ominous."

"It kind of is," Austin admitted. "Brad called me about an hour ago. It seems tomorrow morning I will be getting a visit from Agent Belmont."

"Who's that?"

"The FBI agent who has been investigating Charity's disappearance."

"Why would Brad know about that?" Cinnamon asked.

"He has a buddy at the local FBI office who gave him the heads-up."

"Why is he coming?"

"That's the scary part. I don't know. He usually comes out here once a month or when one of Charity's family members tells a crazy false story about my relationship with Charity. But this time, there's been nothing in the press. No chatter about someone who thought they saw Charity or a tip that came over the hotline. Nothing. That makes me nervous. However, Brad told me there has been a lot of activity and he won't tell me what that is. He says he can't this time, but he said it's potentially bad."

"Does this agent act as if he thinks you did something to her?"

"He did in the beginning. Now he goes back and forth between it either being me or Tom. It's like he plays us off each other. One day he's all friendly with me, telling me he believes it's Tom and not me, the next it's the opposite. He has a job to do, and I get he has to follow all the leads. Brad keeps telling me that if he honestly believed I had anything to do with her disappearance, he'd be coming around more often."

"Do you think Tom did something to her?" Cinnamon asked.

"I used to, but not anymore. He's just as

distraught over her disappearance as I am. Actually, even more. I think the man loved her. I just wanted you to know that this agent will be showing up tomorrow to have a little chat with me."

"I'm glad you told me. It would have totally freaked me out if he randomly knocked on the door and I didn't know."

He took her chin with his thumb and forefinger, giving her little kiss. "Let's finish this amazing dinner. Then I'll do the dishes while you take a nice hot bath. After that, we can watch a movie and go to bed."

"I like that sound of that."

So did Austin.

Now matter how much Cinnamon tried, she couldn't settle her mind. Granted, it had only been twenty minutes since they had climbed into bed. Every night she slept with her back to Austin's chest and his arms around her body. He would whisper good night in her ear and kiss her shoulder. But when she woke in the morning, she'd be alone. He'd always managed to slip from the bed without waking her and jump in the shower. She had no idea why it bothered her so much, but it did.

She rolled to face him, resting her knee on his legs.

He blinked. "Is something wrong?"

"I can't sleep."

Palming her cheek, he leaned in and brushed his lips over her mouth. His kisses were always tender and loving, his embrace protective and warm. She could feel his love with every touch.

But not his passion.

"I know you're worried about things with Pete and the FBI agent coming. I am too. But close your eyes and think about—"

"It's not that." She ran her hand down his chest, letting her fingers graze across his nipples. She moved over his taut stomach and fingered the elastic of his underwear. She didn't dare reach inside. That would be too bold. Too forward. She would allow him to move things along. He had to want it too.

He grabbed her wrist. "What are you doing?"

"I feel like another weight was lifted tonight by you knowing everything that happened and that it allows us to take the next step in our relationship."

He smoothed her hair from her face and stared intently into her eyes. "There's no rush."

"Don't you want me?" She resented the quiver in her voice. She hated how Pete had stolen all her confidence. She'd never had the chance to grow as a woman. She'd been stuck in a cycle of constant fear and denigration.

But not anymore. It wasn't just being back with Austin that gave her strength. She would admit that he helped her pave the way and showed her exactly who she wanted to be. But so did everyone else on Whiskey Ranch. The supportive environment made it easier for her to heal quickly both physically and emotionally. There was no judgment. No one responded negatively. Everyone was happy to have her home.

However, in her heart of hearts, she knew Austin was her soulmate. He was her everything. Not a day had passed that she hadn't thought about him and what he might be doing. Had he married? Did he have children? She had missed him terribly. Now that she could start over, she didn't want to let another night pass.

"Of course I do." He pulled her tight, running his hand up and down her back, gently squeezing her ass. "Don't ever question my desire for you. It takes a lot of restraint and many cold showers to stay here each night and keep my hands to myself. I don't want you to rush into this. You've been through so much and you've barely even left him. You have a lot to work through. I don't want you to regret being with me."

She cupped his face, running a finger over his lower lip. Never in a million years would she have thought he would be concerned about something like that. "I would never. I love you."

"I know you do. But—"

She hushed him with a kiss. She slipped her tongue between his lips, twirling it frantically around his, desperate to show him how ready she was. Feeling empowered, she rolled him to his back, straddling him. She pressed her hands on his chest and sat up taller.

His chest heaved up and down.

She ripped her shirt over her head and tossed it across the room. Taking his hand, she placed it over her breast. Pressure grew between her legs. Her muscles ignited with joy.

His thumb fanned across her nipple. It tightened and tingled.

She arched her back, letting the sensations take over.

"Cinnamon," Austin said with a raspy voice. "Before we continue, I need something from you."

She lowered her gaze. "What?" Her lungs burned. She couldn't fill them.

"I need you to be in control. We do this your way. Whatever you want. How you want it. If you don't like something, we stop. If you're uncomfortable, you tell me and we stop. I need you to promise me that you won't continue just because you think it's what I want."

She couldn't love this man more if she tried. "I promise."

Lifting his head, he took her nipple into his mouth, keeping his eyes locked with hers. He swirled his tongue over the sensitive nub and then sucked.

Running her fingers through his hair, she watched him go from one breast to the other. He teased her relentlessly and she loved every second.

He glided his fingers down the center of her chest, across her stomach, and into her panties. "I want to touch you."

"Oh, God. Yes, please."

He chuckled, lifting her off his lap and gently laying her on the bed. He tugged her underwear down and kissed her ankles. "You're so beautiful."

He licked two fingers before gliding them up her inner thighs. Gently, he rubbed them across her, teasing her, toying with her until she jerked her hips upward, demanding he give her what she desired.

"Please don't hold back." She could barely manage a full breath. "I need you."

He nestled his head between her legs. His tongue darted from his mouth, licking her hard, throbbing nub.

Immediately her body exploded like fireworks going off on the Fourth of July. She dug her heels into the mattress and stared at Austin in awe. She'd never felt more loved in her life.

He reached his hands up and fondled her breasts, tugging and twisting at her nipples.

"Oh my God. Austin," she cried out. An unexpected orgasm tore through her body. She jerked and quivered uncontrollably. She clutched at his head, squeezing her legs together.

Austin continued to lap at her slowly. He inserted two fingers, stroking her tenderly.

The sensation repeated itself two more times, although not as intensely as the first.

He lifted his head, kissing his way up her stomach, stopping at her breasts to suck on her nipples before landing on her lips.

Wrapping her arms around his strong shoulders, she drew him close.

"Are you okay?" he whispered.

"I can't believe you just asked me that question. Isn't it obvious?"

He chuckled. "Yeah. It is. But I'm trying to be a nice guy."

"You can do that by seeing if we can make that happen again." She reached down, slipping her hands into his boxers and pulling them over his ass. "But first I have to see if you're ready."

His brows shot up. "Trust me. I'm more than ready."

"I'll be the judge of that." She pushed him to his back and his boxers to his ankles. It had been a long time since she had enjoyed sex. She ran her hands up his legs, cupping him, stroking him, enjoying how he tensed and relaxed.

"You don't need to do this."

"I want to." She smiled before taking the tip into her mouth.

He groaned, taking her hair and piling it up on top of her head. "You've got two minutes. That's all I can handle."

"Sucks to be a man and not have the ability to have multiples."

"I'm a giver, not a taker."

She stared into his soulful eyes as she licked his shaft.

"Now you only have a minute," he said behind a tight jaw.

Wanting to put that time to good use, she took as much of him into her mouth as she could. Austin had been the first man she'd ever touched. He taught her about his body and showed her things about herself she had no idea about. They had learned to love together. The thrill of being back in his arms filled her heart. There was no other man for her.

Only Austin.

He tugged at her hair. "That's enough."

"I thought you said I was in control."

"You are, except for that." He cupped the back of her neck and kissed her hard. It was filled with passion and made her come alive.

She felt desirable for the first time in years.

Straddling him, she eased his length inside, taking him glorious inch at a time. He filled her like no one else.

He gripped her hips. A groan escaped his mouth.

She rocked back and forth, letting the pressure

build. Her muscles twitched and tightened as her climax approached. She curled her toes, hoping to ward it off, but the pleasure exploded like a volcano.

"Austin. Yes." She pressed her hands on his chest, arching her back, grinding against him with fury. Every nerve ending tingled. Her orgasm rolled into a second as he thrust himself deep inside her, releasing his own.

"Sweet Cinnamon," he whispered, pulling her to his chest and kissing her neck. He ran his hands up and down her back, massaging gently.

It took a good five minutes for either of them to catch their breath.

She rolled off him and snuggled into his side. Tickling her fingers through the few strands of chest hair he had, she sighed. "You're so wonderful."

"So are you." He pressed his lips against her temple. "I love you so much."

She lifted her head. "I love you too. Thank you."

He chuckled. "You never have to thank me for loving you."

"It's not that." She rested her chin on her hands. "You're always so patient and kind." A tear burned her cheek.

"Don't cry, babe."

"These are happy tears." She smiled. "I was so lost when I came here and now I have direction. I truly feel like the world is at my fingertips and everything will be all right."

"It will be." He rubbed his thumb over her lip. "But we might have a problem."

"What's that?"

"Are you on birth control? We didn't discuss that."

Her eyes went wide. "I was, but I left all my pills back in Idaho Falls. I haven't taken them since I arrived and I just didn't think about it."

"I should have been the one who did. Not you." He brushed her hair back. "I'm sorry." His eye twitched. "Would you ever want to have another child?"

"Wow. I don't know. I mean, obviously not in my past situation, but I'd always thought it would be you and me having a family." She dropped her head to his stomach. Her cheeks heated. "I used to fantasize about it late at night or when writing in my journal."

"You wrote about that?" He lifted her chin. "And Pete read it? That couldn't have gone over well."

"Let's not talk about him or what he did with that information." A flash of one of the worst beatings, outside of the last one, she'd ever taken filled her mind.

"Fair enough." Austin nodded.

"Do you want to have kids?"

"I never wanted to have them with anyone but you."

"What about Charity? Did she want them?" Cinnamon asked.

"She did and we talked about it, but it wasn't something that I was fully on board with. I used coming back to Whiskey Ranch as one of the conditions in having a family, which looking back was a mean thing to do."

"You didn't love her."

"No, I didn't." He brushed his warm lips over hers in a tender kiss. "I've always loved you and if I'm being honest, while I don't think this is the right time for us to be reckless about birth control, I want a future with you, including having a family."

"There's still so much that is hanging over my head."

"I know. That's why from now on, I'll reach for a condom."

"You have some?"

"I bought them the other day." He laughed. "I like to be prepared. I've been hoping that someday soon you'd be ready to be open about everything that happened and we could move things along."

"I'm a lucky girl to have such a sweet man in my life."

"No, I'm the lucky one. Now let's get some sleep." He wrapped his arms around her and closed his eyes.

There were only three things that worried Cinnamon.

How long her divorce would take.

How long Pete would end up in prison for.

And what this FBI agent wanted to discuss with Austin.

She sucked in a long shallow breath, letting it out slowly. As if all those worries weren't enough.

*A*ustin leaned against the railing, sipping his coffee and watching the sunrise. He hadn't slept well, which bothered him because he should have, considering how the evening ended. Being with Cinnamon again had been beyond his wildest dreams. It was as if they'd picked up where they left off. They'd been so young. He had been only twenty-one and she nineteen. They'd both suffered great tragedy in their lives. She handled hers well, but Austin had gone to a dark place and he'd lost the woman he loved.

He had only himself to blame for the last fifteen years.

Well, and Pete.

Last night should have marked a new beginning.

A fresh start. Their love was even deeper than before, yet this black cloud hung over his head, waiting to be unleashed. There had been only two other times that Agent Belmont showed up without a story popping up in the news. The first time there had been an anonymous tip that someone had seen Austin dumping what looked like it could have been a body. There was absolutely no truth to it and after Belmont investigated, it turned out to be nothing. According to Belmont, that piece of information was going to be kept from the press and for about a month, there was no talk of it. But someone leaked it and Belmont had to comment.

It made Austin look as though he'd done something to Charity because of the close proximity to the ranch, but no body had ever been found. However, people still talked.

Which didn't help Austin in the court of public opinion.

The second time was when some random woman came forward, stating she saw Austin driving Charity's vehicle near the same location. That was damning because this woman was adamant and had a clear description. But there was not enough evidence to bring Austin up on charges.

Yet.

His cell buzzed. He glanced at the screen.

Tom.

In the last few months, they'd become friendly.

"Hey, Tom, what's up?"

"Have you gotten a visit from Belmont?"

"I'm expecting him this morning, why?" Austin asked.

"I know we don't always see eye to eye on things, but I have a bad feeling about this."

"I take it you've spoken to Belmont."

"He paid me a visit last night and asked me all sorts of questions like if I knew about any connections Charity might have had with a Pete and Cinnamon Thompson."

"What the fuck?" Austin dropped the phone. He bent over and picked up, hitting the speaker button and planting his butt on the steps. "Are you shitting me?"

"Nope. He asked me if Charity could have been speaking with either of them."

"That's fucked up." Austin swallowed. "But is it possible she could have known Pete?"

"When I look back on the last few months of the affair, I wonder why she moved there with you. I begged her not to. Please don't take this the wrong way and I don't say it to hurt you."

"We're past all that, Tom."

"Okay. Okay. She kept complaining to me about how much she didn't love you and hated the idea of living there. Once she got to the ranch, it was even worse. I didn't understand why she did it if she wanted to be with me. She kept saying she owed it to you and I thought, not if she didn't love you. So, if this Pete guy wanted to take you down for some reason, and she knew it, anything is possible."

"Holy shit." Austin jumped to his feet and raced into the house. "Cinnamon, I need your cell."

"Cinnamon's there?" Tom asked.

"Yeah. It's a long story, but if my suspicions are right, there's a timeline, and we might finally have some answers. Can I call you back?"

"Please do, but also, watch your back. And for the record, I'm sorry if I did anything to perpetuate this vendetta against you. I'll also do whatever it takes to help."

"I might just have to take you up on that," Austin said. "I'll be in touch." He stared at Cinnamon who stood in the kitchen wearing his old football jersey and boxers.

He groaned.

"Why do you need this?" She placed her phone in his hands.

"Did you delete anything from Pete or from me over the last year and a half?"

"You told me not to in case we needed it in the divorce or his criminal trial."

"Good girl." He batted her nose. "I can't believe I didn't see this sooner."

"What are you talking about?" Cinnamon asked.

"The timing of when we started talking. Charity moving here. Her disappearance. And someone trying to frame me."

Austin's heart pounded out of control. He paced on the porch, glancing at his watch every couple of minutes. Yesterday, he had no desire to speak with Belmont.

Now he couldn't wait, he couldn't wait.

"You need to relax." Cinnamon stepped from the house and handed him a tall glass of lemonade. "Not only are you going to put a hole in those floorboards, but it's not going to make this guy show up any faster."

He set the glass on the small table next to the Adirondack chairs. "A million things are running through my brain and none are good."

Cinnamon pointed down the long dirt road. "Is that him?"

"Looks that way." Austin wiggled his fingers. "Why don't you go inside for a while."

"I didn't take the day off work to sit on the sidelines." She planted her hands on her hips. "Don't push me away because you believe I can't handle what you're thinking."

"It's not that." He inched closer, curling his fingers around her forearms. "I just don't want him to question you."

"Why not? Maybe I know something but I'm not aware that I do."

Shit, that made way too much logical sense. However, he still didn't like the idea. Not until after he learned why Belmont had made the trip. The secretiveness about this haunted him. "That's possible, but I want to talk to him alone first. It has nothing to do with hiding anything from you or not believing you can handle it. I want to understand what he has or doesn't have before sharing my thoughts. I need to know what's going on and Brad won't or can't tell me."

"Fine." She spun on her heel and stormed off into the house.

Fuck. That's not how he wanted her to respond. He stuffed his hands in his pockets and stared at the approaching vehicle. Glancing over his shoulder, his heart ached. He hated that he'd hurt Cinnamon's feelings. All he wanted to do was protect and shield her from what could be coming. Brad had warned him that the moment Belmont came unannounced could be the time he came with either a warrant to search or one to arrest. This situation was ripe for disaster.

Austin hadn't done anything. However, he was the most logical suspect. He had motive and opportunity.

Tom did as well and had faced similar questioning from Belmont. It wasn't until Tom and Austin decided to stop looking at the other as the bad guy and come together in the search for answers that they realized that Charity had been playing them both. She was only going to stay with whoever would give her the kind of life she wanted.

Austin had more money. He could provide the lifestyle she wanted but refused to lavish her with expensive gifts and let her spend whatever she wanted. However, he did cave on occasion.

The car.

Clothes.

But Tom had status in Boise. He was respected. He owned a business and everyone liked him. He might not have a bank account filled with a couple of million, but he did have the social life that Charity craved. Their love triangle became a contest that he wasn't even aware he'd become a participant in until it was almost too late. But once he had, he'd given her walking papers and because she had her backup, she ran as fast as she could before Tom wised up to her game.

Belmont stepped from his vehicle and adjusted his suit coat. He always showed up in his standard dark suit and black tie. He looked like a typical federal agent. The first time Austin had met him, he'd been terrified, but that emotion came out sideways in sarcasm and frustration.

Not anymore.

"Good morning," Austin said. "It's been a little over a month since you've paid me a visit."

Belmont nodded. "May I join you on the porch and have a little chat?"

"Of course." Austin waved his hand. Most conversations were pleasant enough. It had only been the first two or three that had been extremely uncomfortable, or even painful. Belmont had a dry personality. His tone was even and controlled, but Austin could tell he cared about his job and this case in particular.

Belmont chose one of the Adirondack chairs, so Austin picked the one next to him.

"Shall we get right down to business?" Belmont asked.

"Sure." Austin stretched out his legs, crossing them at the ankles, doing his best to relax. "Do you have any leads?"

"That's why I'm here," Belmont said. "We got an anonymous tip that Charity's car was spotted not far from Whiskey Ranch."

Austin arched a brow but said nothing.

"Does that surprise you?" Belmont asked.

"It does. Especially after all this time." Austin wondered if the question was meant to bait him into a certain reaction. His attorney had told him to answer questions without adding too much, be polite, and stop talking the second he felt as though he were under the microscope. "Did you find it?"

"We did." Belmont leaned forward. "Most of the time, these tips lead us on a wild goose chase. If we do find something, it's not what we expected. Or it doesn't give us a clear picture of what could have happened. This time, we found the vehicle exactly where the tip said it would be."

"Are you going to tell me where that was?" Austin sat up taller. His heart hit his throat. Poor Charity. Whatever happened to her, she had to be terrified and that broke his heart into a million pieces. He'd failed her like he'd done so many other people in his life. Just because he didn't love her or want to be with her anymore, didn't mean he wished her harm.

"Five miles from the ranch. It was driven off a dirt road and hidden in a field." Belmont held Austin's gaze. "We're going to take the car to our lab today."

"When did you find it and how did we not know about it?" Austin made sure he kept his tone even. "Also, should I have my attorney present now?" He waved his cell. "Because if that's the case, he's ten minutes out and we'll need to put this conversation on hold." The one thing Austin had always been able to count on when it came to Belmont had been honesty about when Ted should be at his side.

This felt slightly different.

Belmont rubbed his chin with his thumb and forefinger, glancing at the sky. "I'm stuck between a rock and a hard place here. This case has been ice-cold for months. Every tip we get always points to you, yet it always comes up like I'm chasing my tail. This is the first time the anonymous caller's information had any teeth. But I find the timing of it very suspicious."

"What do you mean?"

"I didn't show you this." Belmont tapped his screen, holding it up for Austin to see. "This was sent the same day we got the tip, two days ago."

Austin clenched his fists as he watched the interaction between him and Pete at Boone's bar. It showed a little different story than what actually happened. The version that had been shared with Belmont portrayed Austin as the aggressor, not Pete.

Fucking artificial intelligence.

"You should know this was posted to social media as of this morning," Belmont said. "My boss is hot for me to wrap this case up now that we have Charity's car."

"This was altered. I can produce many witnesses."

"That's not necessary. I took the time to do some digging before I came out here. I didn't want to question you without a bigger picture, so I contacted some key witnesses and they painted a much different story." Belmont held up his hand.

"Right now, I don't want you to answer any questions or tell me anything. Not without your lawyer and that's not because I think you had anything to do with Charity's disappearance. I've been doing this job a long time and some things have me sniffing in a different direction. But again, my boss is ready to pounce on you, so I have to play along a little bit. I also want to make sure the investigation is protected as well as you."

"I appreciate your vote of confidence, especially since in the beginning I thought you believed I did something to her."

"I'm not sure I ever thought that, but I had to consider the possibility." Belmont leaned back. "I will have to go through the process. Ask you all the tough questions—with your lawyer present—and I need to interview Cinnamon Thompson." He lifted his thumb and motioned to the house.

"First, she's changing her name back to Whiskey the first chance she gets. Secondly, why? And finally, what makes you think she's here?"

Belmont laughed. "I can't tell you why now, so I need a little trust from you, and come on, man. She was in that video, which is in the forensics lab, so if it was doctored, we'll figure that out. But she's your ex-girlfriend and I've done my homework. She's the love of your life and everyone in this town is rooting for the two of you to get back together. Hell, after hearing the stories, I'm even hoping it happens."

"You're not talking to her without a lawyer or me present."

"Lawyer is fine, but you will not be there. Sorry. That would be mudding waters, and I can't afford to do that."

"Can you at least tell my why—outside of that video—you need to converse with Cinnamon?"

"Nope."

"I might have an ounce of trust for you, but I don't for your profession," Austin said.

"Ouch." Belmont tapped his chest. "I'm sure you don't feel that way about your brother-in-law."

"Oh, we've had our differences of opinion a time or two." Austin understood how the legal system worked but didn't often agree with it. "Here comes Ted." Ted Rosen had worked as JW's lawyer since his situation with his ex-fiancée a few years ago but had also done contract work as needed for Whiskey Ranch before that. He was a good man and Austin wished he didn't need his services. "Shall we do all this now?"

"I'd rather get through as much as I can, but I will have more questions as we process the vehicle."

Austin waved Ted up. They were way past formalities, considering Austin had to constantly call him last minute to come out and handle this situation with Belmont. "Thanks for coming out."

"Sure thing." Ted stretched out his hand and shook both men's hands. "I drove past a crew of local police and Feds pulling out a vehicle from the deep off the side of the road. Is that why I'm here?"

This was one of the reasons Austin appreciated Ted. He got right down to business and he didn't sugarcoat things.

"That's one of them," Belmont said.

"What does that have to do with my client?" Ted asked.

"A number of things, beginning with the registration matches Charity's car. The proximity of the ranch. The fact that we found two items that we believe belong to Austin and—"

"What items?" Ted asked.

One of the many things Austin liked about Ted was that he didn't let anything go by without demanding further explanation. He didn't wait for anyone to finish their statement before digging for what he wanted to know. It often caused a rift between him and law enforcement, but that was the nature of the beast.

"A pair of men's gloves, which have blood on them, and a belt with a Whiskey Ranch buckle much like the one he's wearing now." Belmont lifted his finger. "None of this is being released to the press."

"Ted, am I allowed to speak freely?" Austin glanced at his lawyer.

Ted nodded.

"I'm not missing a belt. However, a few weeks ago, Gage borrowed a pair of my gloves."

"I'll need to speak to Gage," Belmont said.

"He's visiting his brothers in Twin City. He left a few days ago and we haven't heard from him since he departed." Austin didn't want to bring Gage into any of this. He'd been through enough in his life. The loss of his family had tormented Gage for years. The dirty looks from the community because so many people believed he started the fire, which had been proven false, but that didn't stop the gossip.

Gage was on the spectrum and many people didn't understand what that meant. They viewed him as strange and off-putting, when in reality he was the kindest, sweetest man on the planet.

"I'd like his contact information," Belmont said.

"I'm happy to give it to you, but you need to

understand that Gage has some social issues. You can't come at him like you would anyone else." Austin leaned forward. "When you speak to him, it would be better if someone from this ranch—someone he trusts—is with you; otherwise, he's going to panic."

"I've spoken to him a couple of times. He's very protective of you and everyone else on this ranch. I understand his personality and promise to handle the situation appropriately. However, I have to consider what you just told me about the gloves and the fact that Gage made it very clear he couldn't stand Charity. I'm also aware he wasn't a fan of Pete. Is that because of Cinnamon? Because I get there is more to that story and now I want to know why."

"It mostly has to do with Cinnamon, but Pete did date his daughter before she died. Pete didn't care about her. It was all to stay close to Cinnamon and Gage took it personally because it hurt Alyssa, but shortly after that, the fire happened." Austin shook his head. "There is no way in hell Gage would have done anything to hurt Charity, no matter his feelings. He might wear his emotions on his sleeve and he can occasionally say things that are socially inappropriate, but he doesn't have a violent bone in his body."

"As opposed to you." Belmont lowered his chin.

"I don't pretend to be a saint. However, I've never once laid a hand on a woman." Austin was so tired of this never-ending cycle. He wanted Charity to be safe, but deep down in his soul, he knew that wasn't the case. It had been too long since she disappeared for that to be true.

Now all he wanted was answers and for whoever had harmed her to be locked up where they belonged.

But it wasn't Gage.

"Are you willing to give a DNA sample?" Belmont asked.

Ted waved his hand. "If you find DNA in the vehicle, we'll have that conversation, but I'm not going to allow my client to give it now."

"Fair enough," Belmont said. "Now I want to talk about this video." He handed Ted his cell. "Austin had indicated he believes it was doctored. I have spoken to the owner of Boone's Bar and Grill and a Ms. Welch as well as those she had dined with along with five other people I've been able to track down that were at Boone's that evening. I've spoken with the local sheriff. They have all given me the same story, which doesn't quite match up to that video."

Ted handed the phone back. "I'm not sure what this has to do with Charity's disappearance."

"I can't get into the details of the possible connection other than we got an anonymous tip the next day," Belmont said.

"Still don't get it." Ted arched a brow.

"I want to know more about your relationship with Pete Thompson." Belmont held Austin's gaze. "Let's start with how long have you known him?"

Austin glanced to Ted.

"Go ahead and answer," Ted said.

"Most of my life. He grew up here in Buhl. We went to the same high school." Austin had been trained to keep his answers short and to the point, so he left it at that.

"Were you friends?" Belmont asked.

"Nope." Austin folded his arms. Any conversation about Pete tended to put him on the defensive.

"Why not?" Belmont took out his notebook and pen.

"In part because he had a thing for Cinnamon," Austin said.

"She was your high school sweetheart, correct?" Belmont thumbed through his pad. He knew all this, so why he had to ask was beyond Austin.

"We were best friends and then became boyfriend and girlfriend," Austin said.

"Was there any other reason you didn't get along with Pete?" Belmont asked.

"Sure," Austin admitted. "He was the kind of guy who thought he was better than the rest of us, especially anyone who thought being a rancher was a good way to make a living. His parents were divorced and he lived here with his mom who had married a man who worked at a neighboring ranch. Pete hated it and couldn't wait to get the hell out and go work for his dad. That's exactly what he did. He's used money and power to get whatever he wants."

"Is it safe to say that you and Pete have butted heads for as long as you've known him?" Belmont asked. "And have you been in any physical altercations with him?"

"It's common knowledge that we don't like each other and yes, we've been in a few brawls both in high school and once right before he and Cinnamon married," Austin said. "Can you please tell me where you're going with this?"

"Not yet." Belmont glanced up. "Does Pete know Tom? Or did he know Charity?"

Austin thought he'd been prepared for this question, but hearing it made the acid in his stomach lurch to his throat. "I don't believe so."

"But is it possible?" Belmont set his notebook aside.

"I suppose. However, I don't see how or why," Austin said. But he did. Only, he wasn't willing to be the one to verbalize that thought. That needed to come from someone else.

Ted leaned forward. "Are you suggesting that Pete could be setting Austin up to take the fall for Charity's disappearance? Is there something I need to know to help my client navigate this new territory you're heading in? Or is there new evidence I should have?"

"Even if that were the case, you know I couldn't express that as the lead investigator in this case. Not while actively asking the questions." Belmont tilted his head.

"Should we break out a beer and chat like old buddies?" Ted lowered his chin.

"Right now, everything I'm thinking is based on hunches and half information," Belmont said. "Remember, my boss is gunning for Austin, but I'm taking a little different approach. Please let me do my job and have a little faith that I want truth and justice. This is more than wrapping up a case and getting it off my desk. I don't want to see an innocent man go down for something he didn't do. But I also don't want to rush anything."

"I can live with that," Ted said. "But you're forcing us to fly blind here, and I don't like that. Austin has been through enough."

"I agree." Belmont sighed. "Now, I really need to speak with Cinnamon and I know she's inside."

"You're not doing that without me present," Ted said. "So, I need to have her hire me." He stood. "Let me go take care of that. In the meantime, Austin, don't answer anything else officially."

"I know the drill." Austin leaned back and watched Ted stroll across the porch and into the house. A theory formed in Austin's head, and he didn't like it one bit.

Cinnamon resented that Austin couldn't be present. He'd become her rock. Her safety net. She felt like she could get through anything when he was around. It wasn't that she didn't believe in herself. Being home had given her strength. Her family had wrapped their loving arms around her without question or judgment. She knew she could continue on her path because she had the support she needed.

Austin added a different element to her world. He was her future. A partner in life. Someone she could confide in. Trust. Love.

She fiddled with her fingernails and glanced between Ted and Belmont. Ted told her that he'd remain quiet unless necessary.

"I only have a few questions for you," Agent Belmont said. "Did your husband ever mention Charity or Tom's name to you?"

"No," she said, taking the advice of Ted and keeping her answers direct.

"Did your husband travel for work?"

"He did," she said.

"Did he ever travel to Boise?" Belmont asked.

"A few times a year."

"What about Twin City?"

"He went there too," she admitted.

"Does your husband have a second cell phone?" Belmont asked.

Her heart dropped to the pit of her stomach. "I believe so. I mean, I've seen him with one and when I asked him about it, he told me it was none of my business." She rubbed her cheek. "And then proceeded to hit me." She decided tossing that piece of information out there was okay.

"I'm sorry that happened to you." Belmont's expression softened. "Could your husband have gone places and done things you wouldn't have known?"

"Absolutely."

"Can you please explain to me how that is possible?" Belmont asked.

In the past, her shame would interfere with her ability to be honest, but not anymore. "It was an abusive marriage and Pete was incredibly controlling. When he left for work in the morning, he shut down the internet, then took the car keys and all my credit cards. I've left him, which is why I'm here."

"Was he always like that?"

She shook her head. "The first few years weren't horrible. It wasn't until after our daughter died that things changed. It was difficult for us, and he didn't handle it well." She held up her hand. "I'm not making excuses for what he did, especially considering how bad it got. However, it was a slow progression and I found myself trapped in a situation I didn't know how to get out of."

"That's usually how it happens." Belmont nodded.

Cinnamon glanced at her watch. It was still before noon. All she could focus on was Pete's hearing. She should be more concerned about this visit from Belmont and what that meant for Austin.

And she was. The last thing she needed was more drama or for something bad to happen to Austin.

But she couldn't deal with the idea that Pete could be released from jail. He believed he was above the law and wouldn't hesitate to return to Buhl to collect what he believed was his property.

"Cinnamon, is it safe to say that your husband would do anything to ensure Austin was out of your life?"

"Not just Austin, but my family too. He didn't like how close we all used to be. Pete did whatever he could to cut me off from them and sadly, I allowed it."

"What about Gage?"

"Gage?" She tilted her head. "What does he have to do anything?"

"I'm not sure. However, I understand he had a soft spot for you and hated Charity."

"I wouldn't know anything about Charity. I never met her, but yes. Gage and I have a special bond. I was quite close to his daughter, Alyssa. She was on the spectrum—like Gage—and got bullied a fair amount in school from the popular crowd."

"Did Pete bully her? Austin told me they dated in high school."

Cinnamon laughed. "I'm not sure you could call it that. Pete hung around her as a way to get close to me. He had it in his head it would make me jealous. It didn't. If anything, it made me mad because I never once believed he cared for her.

After the fire that killed her, her two brothers, and her mom, Pete did his best to use that to console me, but I had Austin."

"I read the fire report. It says that a cigarette started it in one of the boys' rooms," Belmont said.

Cinnamon closed her eyes. "I've always found that hard to believe. Her older brothers chewed tobacco but they never smoked."

"But her father did, is that correct?" Belmont asked.

"He'd quit a year before and I've never seen him light up after that. No one has."

Belmont flipped through his pad. "Pete stated in his interview that Alyssa confided in him that she'd not only seen her father smoke, but he'd gotten drunk and had a horrible fight with her mother that day."

"Gage has never raised his voice in all the years that I've known him," Cinnamon said. "And he's not a drinker. He might have a beer or a glass of whiskey with the crew, but never more than one."

"I'm seeing an intriguing pattern in this questioning," Ted spoke for the first time since the interview began.

She'd almost forgotten he was there.

"It's as if you're implying two things," Ted said.

"And what's that?" Belmont arched a brow.

"That Pete might have had something to do with the fire that killed Gage's family and that he could have had a hand in the disappearance of Charity," Ted said. "Why are you being so cagey about this? Austin has never done anything but cooperate with this investigation. Cinnamon is now doing the same thing. I would appreciate a little color here."

"All I have is a working theory with absolutely no facts to back it up." Belmont held up his hand. "I need a lot more information before I can even call Pete a person of interest. The only thing I have is that the tips come from a phone in Boise."

Ted sucked on his teeth. "Why didn't you tell Austin this?"

"Because I can't have him go off half-cocked, and we both know that's exactly what he'll do," Belmont said.

"Not with me here, he won't." Cinnamon stood and planted her hands on her hips. "We have a second chance and he's not going to do anything that will jeopardize that. Pete has a hearing in three hours. If he—"

"Trust me. I'm aware of that hearing and here's the problem. I'm told the judge overseeing that case doesn't have a stellar reputation—as in he's taken bribes before—but it's never been proven. I'm on a time crunch here to raise a flag that Pete could be involved. I know Austin and I can't have him getting in my way."

"Keeping shit from Austin isn't the way to do it," Ted said. "Or me for that matter. You need to use us."

"I can't. That will taint the case. I've already told you too much." Belmont tucked his notebook into his suit pocket.

"I've got an idea." Cinnamon inched toward the picture window. She stared at Austin who paced in the yard by the oak tree. "It's going to take a lot of convincing to get Austin to go along with it, but if Pete is behind this, he's arrogant enough to tell me about it."

"Excuse me?" Belmont said.

She turned. "Pete has always used fear to control me. After our daughter died and he started hitting me, I told him I would leave. I was stronger back then and wasn't going to stand for it. I had even packed my bags. But when Pete came home from a business trip, he'd brought something that belonged to Georgia Moon. He told me that if he could slip into her room at night and steal that, he could do whatever he wanted."

"Jesus," Belmont muttered. "He admitted to breaking into her home?"

Cinnamon nodded. "Pete threatened to ruin—or hurt—my family. It started as little things. Exposing family secrets. Or making up lies that he'd make stick. He beat me down emotionally and physically until I believed everything he told me. Plus, I knew his threats were real." She blew out a long breath. "He once told me he was the one who made all the horses sick at Whiskey Ranch when Austin first started working. There were other things too, like feeding Bella—JW's ex-fiancée—information about him to use against him after they broke up. If I stayed with him, he promised to leave them alone. I had minimal contact with my family, so I hadn't heard the stories or read the headlines until Pete showed them to me each time I threatened him that I would leave. I didn't even know Bella existed until after JW dumped her."

"What exactly are you suggesting?" Ted asked.

"If he gets out of jail, let him come. He'll enjoy telling me what he did to this family. And if he did set fire to Gage's house, I'll get him to admit that too." She sucked in a deep breath. "I'm the only one who can get him to admit it."

"All while he's beating the crap out of you." Ted jumped to his feet. "Not only won't I let you do this, but Austin will go ballistic."

"It's not Austin's decision. It's mine." She held Ted's gaze.

"And if he's not released?" Belmont asked.

"I'll go to him," she said. "This is not up for debate. It's the only way to find out if he had any connection to Charity or to Gage's family. We all want answers. Let's get them."

"No fucking way. Nope. Not happening. Over my goddamned dead body." Austin stood in the kitchen and stared at Cinnamon with shock and horror in his heart. "You've lost your mind."

"I'm thinking clearly for the first time since my daughter died." She held his gaze with a fierce determination that he hadn't seen in years.

Austin turned and raked a hand through his thick hair.

"Brad said—"

Austin interrupted Cinnamon. "You called my

brother-in-law?" He turned on his heel and pointed to Ted. "Did you know about this?"

Ted nodded. "I suggested it."

"You've got to be fucking kidding me." He took in a slow calming breath when all he wanted to do was put his fist through a wall. He should have known something was up the second Belmont asked him to walk him to his vehicle and then told him absolutely nothing of importance. "It's one thing to call the bastard, but I'm not letting him walk onto this ranch, much less spend any time alone with you. It's insanity. Hell, it's a death wish."

Cinnamon eased closer. She rested her soft hand on his forearm. Her touch calmed his soul but didn't ease his fears. "The one thing Pete wants more than anything is to control me. In order to do that, he needs to make me believe he still has power over me. That he can hurt me. The only way he can do that now is to prove to me he's already done horrible things and will continue if I don't return to Idaho Falls."

Austin ran his thumb over her cheek. "Hasn't he caused you enough pain?"

"He's done that to all of us," she whispered. "But I'll have the upper hand. I won't be alone. Brad will have this place bugged. Or wherever I end up meeting him. He will have his people there and Belmont promised he'd have some of his men—people Pete doesn't know—there as well. He won't be able to lay a finger on me and I'll be able to get him to tell me everything."

"Why can't I do it?" Austin asked.

"Because you won't be able to control your temper," Ted said.

"Not to mention he doesn't want to control you and keep you to himself." Cinnamon ran her hand up and down Austin's arm. "I'd be more afraid he'd kill you than me."

Austin audibly growled. "I don't know about that. I saw what you looked like the night you showed up here."

"That's because I filed for divorce. Because I said I was coming back here and he knew you were single and still living on the ranch. If he believes there's a chance I'll come back to him or that he can win, he's not going to do that kind of damage." She leaned in and kissed his cheek. "If he killed Charity and is trying to frame you, it's all about getting you out of the picture. I'm the trophy and he won't hesitate to put you six feet into the ground. It's time to beat him at his own game."

"She makes sense," Ted said. "It's not the

perfect plan, but if he's released from jail, we all know he's coming here anyway. We might as well be prepared to nail his ass to the wall once and for all and end this."

Austin pulled Cinnamon to his chest. "I don't know what I'd do if I ever lost you again."

"Let's make sure that doesn't happen." She rested her head on his shoulder. "I'm worried about Gage, though. What if he did something to him? The timing of when he left to go see people he hasn't seen since his family died and when Pete showed up is unusual to say the least."

He kissed her temple. "Belmont is looking into it. So is JW." He squeezed his eyes. "I will go along with this plan, but only if I can be part of it."

"Brad isn't going to like that," Ted said. "But I did get him to agree to make sure you were in on everything, and he wouldn't dare ask you to sit on the sidelines simply because he wouldn't if this were his wife."

Austin had to love his brother-in-law.

"I need to get going," Ted said. "Call me when you know what's going on and Cinnamon, make sure this guy keeps his cool."

"I will." She pulled from Austin's embrace. "Thank you for everything."

"I'm looking forward to getting to know you better once all this is over." Ted smiled. "I'll see myself out."

Austin reached for a mug and made his third cup of coffee for the day. "Would you like one?"

"I'll float away if I have more." She climbed up on one of the stools.

While he didn't feel great about the plan, he knew it was the only way. However, his heart still remained firmly wedged in his throat. The mere idea of her confronting Pete made his skin crawl. Worse, the fact that he could have been responsible for Alyssa and her brothers' deaths made him want to strangle the man himself. Poor Gage had been accused of killing his family. He'd lived with the stares and cruel looks from the town for years. Even he'd wondered if he'd been sneaking cigarettes and never told anyone out of shame. But he knew him well enough that he would have owned up to it and not allowed one of his boys to be blamed for an accidental fire.

"I'm exhausted and it's not even two in the afternoon yet," Cinnamon said.

"I know what you mean." He leaned against the counter. His mind continued to mull over everything he'd learned or pieced together in the last two hours.

"I missed a whole day with the babies and will probably have to miss tomorrow since I won't want to wait there for fucking Pete to show up."

"Nope. We will want to ensure we put as few people as possible in the line of fire." He raised his cup to his lips and sipped. "I still don't like this ridiculous plan all of you came up with behind my back."

"Austin, it wasn't like that."

"It feels that way to me." He set his mug on the island. "But I suppose I can be stubborn and I might have reacted even worse when it was first discussed."

"You have to know this was totally my idea."

He nodded. "While I still don't like it, I do love that you're regaining your confidence and voice and standing up for what you want."

"I will never let another man control me again."

"I guess I came on kind of strong, but all I want is for you to be safe and free of Pete."

"And you want me here with you."

Austin ran a hand over his face. "Isn't that what you want?"

"There are so many things I want and I do

know I can have many of them once I'm out of the clutches of Pete. It will take some hard work on my part, but I can turn my life around." She tucked her hair behind her ears. "I need to go to counseling. I need to have a little time and space to heal."

"What exactly are you saying?"

"I love you." She eased off the chair and made her way around the island.

His chest tightened. Fear gripped his soul. His world hinged on her words. "Why do I feel like there's a but coming?"

"There's not." She palmed his cheek. "We've eased into living together and I haven't wanted to leave because I feel safe from Pete. You protect me from all the bad things on the other side of the ranch fence."

"Isn't that what a boyfriend is supposed to do?"

"Talking out this plan, I realized a part of me doesn't know how to take care of myself. I need to be able to do that. When this is over, I want to ask JW if there is a space that I can move into—by myself—and spend a little time living alone."

"What about us?" He held his breath.

"We will still be together." She wrapped her arms around his shoulders. "I don't want things between us to change, except I can't live here. Not yet."

"I understand." And he did. She'd been only nineteen when she married Pete and became a mom. Nineteen when Pete began to gaslight and control her every move.

Austin had waited fifteen years for her to come to him, he could wait a few more months. He brushed his mouth across her warm lips. "You should live here and I will move into the bunkhouse."

She jerked her head. "With the cowboys?"

He laughed. "The apartment above it is currently empty. It's the only place I know that's available on the ranch and I don't think you want to live there."

"No, I don't. But do you? The cowboys can get pretty rowdy."

"It will be temporary." He kissed her nose. "Because I intend to sweep you off your feet and show you what a great catch I am." He winked.

"I already know that. But what I need to comprehend is that I'm one too."

"I can be a patient man." He pulled her close. He would give her the world if he could. Whatever she wanted because she deserved to have her hopes and dreams fulfilled. He'd deal if it meant sleeping alone for a few more months. "I will do whatever you need because I love you and I want you to be happy."

She sniffled into his shirt.

"Damn, I didn't mean to make you cry." He smoothed his fingers through her long silky hair.

"Your willingness to let me do what I need to makes me want to change my mind."

He cupped her face. "A lot is going on right now. You're in the beginning stages of a divorce. Your husband is facing criminal charges. Not to mention everything we just learned. It's overwhelming for both of us. Settling into a relationship together too quickly might not be the healthiest move. We have lots of time to date and learn about each other and who we are now. I don't want you to think this is me stepping back because it's not. I'm being realistic about the situation."

"You've changed," she said. "For the better. The old you might have taken this as me having second thoughts."

"Even if you were—and I know that's not the case—it would be okay." He pressed his lips over her mouth. "Now, I don't know about you, but I can't sit here and wait for a phone call regarding

Pete's hearing. I'm not that patient. I will lose my freaking mind. So, how about we grab that leftover fried chicken and potato salad, saddle up a couple of horses, and have ourselves a little picnic."

"Sounds like a perfect way to avoid going stir-crazy."

"You pack the basket. I'll go get the horses ready." He patted her bottom. "I'll see you outside. He glanced at his watch as he approached the back door. It could be an hour before the phone call came in.

Or five.

In the meantime, he'd call JD. Everyone at the ranch needed to be prepared for the worst. He also needed to get a handle on where and what Gage was up to. He didn't like that Gage had been MIA. That didn't make sense and he worried that something had happened.

Cinnamon set the basket on the kitchen table. The picnic had been a nice distraction, even though she couldn't eat very much. She had tried forcing down as much as possible, knowing she'd need her strength. If Pete was released from jail, she knew he wouldn't wait long before heading to Buhl. He would view this as a personal attack and he wouldn't take it lying down.

A knock at the door startled her and she jumped, knocking the basket to the floor. "Shit," she mumbled.

Half the contents tumbled out, making a massive mess. Chicken bones, mustard, and the potato container opened.

"Let me see who's at the door, and then I'll help with that." Austin squeezed her shoulder. "I know you're stressed, but this is not a big deal."

She sighed, bending over, then snagged the bones and tossed them in the garbage.

"Austin? Are you here?" a familiar voice rang out.

"In the kitchen," Austin said.

"Wonder what JD wants." Cinnamon took a roll of paper towels and got on her hands and knees. "I can't imagine he's heard about the hearing before we have." Her words were more to herself than Austin.

JD strolled into the kitchen. He smiled, but it was forced. "I just got off the phone with Gage's brother."

Immediately, she stopped what she was doing

and rocked back on her heels. Her heart dropped to her gut.

"And?" Austin asked.

"Gage hasn't been in contact with him, much less scheduled a visit." JD leaned against the counter. "I've already called Brad and filed a missing person's report."

"Jesus." Austin sat on one of the stools. "But Gage texted us." He raked a hand across the top of his head.

Cinnamon leaped to her feet. "Gage supposedly left for his brother's place about when Pete showed up. I bet he had something to do with Gage's disappearance. Pete could have sent that text and since Gage hasn't responded to any call or subsequent text since then, it's what makes the most sense."

"Especially since Pete's been behind bars on and off," JD said.

Cinnamon planted her hands on her hips and paced in front of the island. "If Pete hurt one hair on Gage's head, I'm going to kill him with my bare hands."

Austin stepped in front of her. "Don't say things like that. Someone might think you're being serious."

"What if—"

He hushed her with his finger. "We're all thinking exactly the same things you are. That Pete killed Charity. He killed Gage's family. And now maybe Gage."

"And he's setting you up to take the fall." She glared.

"I'm well aware of what he's trying to do to me, but he's not going to get away with it." Austin lowered his chin. "However, we can't go making threats of murder because if Pete does wind up dead, and anyone has heard us say that, it can be used against us."

She blew out a puff of air. "Fine, but I won't sit around and let him ruin my life anymore. Or anyone I care about. I've been a victim for too long and thanks to me, innocent people have died."

"None of this is your fault," JD said. "I do have to wonder how he managed to get Charity's car out here because that timeline doesn't fit. He was in jail when it showed up."

"He could have paid one of his employees to do it," Cinnamon said. "He has a few loyal ones, although he uses fear and gaslighting to control them too. When people quit his company, he destroys them. He had one nice man working for him a few years ago. But because he dared to question the way Pete ran things, he was put through hell in the press. Some scandal with his wife that turned out wasn't even true."

"We know he was behind some of the shit we've had to deal with over the years," JD said. "We've always had the ability both with money and the fact we've never done anything wrong to come out of whatever was tossed our way."

"But now we're talking possible murder." Austin squeezed her biceps. "And not just Charity." He reached into his back pocket. "This is the call we've been waiting for." He tapped the green button and put it on speaker. "Hey, Belmont. I'm here with Cinnamon and JD Whiskey."

"I just got off the phone with the DA in Idaho Falls. The judge ruled in Pete's favor. He's being released as we speak. He's been warned he's not supposed to leave the county except for business, to which he immediately explained he has a meeting tomorrow in Twin City."

"That's not too far from Buhl," Austin said.

"No, it's not," Belmont agreed. "I'm forty minutes from the ranch. I want to set it up tonight. I'll contact Brad as soon as I end this call."

"You should know that we've filed an official missing person's report on Gage," JD added.

"I've already seen the report and made it part of the FBI investigation. I need Austin's DNA sample as we found blood in the car and on the gloves," Belmont said.

"That makes me nervous since I lent a pair to Gage and it's possible the blood could be mine." Austin rubbed the back of his neck.

"I'm aware," Belmont said. "There is more physical evidence that we have found and we can prove that the car was moved to that location recently."

"How?" Cinnamon asked.

"Eyewitnesses who saw two men put it there. Unfortunately, they don't match Pete's description, but they don't match Austin's either," Belmont said.

"Can you get me a description? I might be able to match them to Pete's employees."

"Already have a forensics artist working on a sketch. Once I have that, I'll let you take a look," Belmont said. "I'll be at Austin's place soon. I suspect that Pete will either come in like a snake before dawn, or he'll contact Cinnamon between now and morning like the arrogant prick he is. Either way, when he does show up, I want to be ready."

"So do we," Austin said. "See you soon." He

wrapped his arms around Cinnamon. "We're going to get him and put him where he belongs. I promise."

"I know you mean that, but Belmont is right about him being a snake. He's gotten away with so many things and I wish I could say I wasn't terrified."

JD stood. "You've got everyone on this ranch behind you. No one will let him ever hurt you or anyone else again. Trust me on that." He leaned in and kissed her cheek. "I'm just sorry we didn't intervene sooner."

"I didn't let you," she said softly.

"Doesn't mean we shouldn't have tried harder." JD nodded. "I'll gather the troops and be back here with everyone in half an hour."

"Sounds like a plan." Austin shook JD's hand.

She squared her shoulders, refusing to let the tears fall this time. This was her home. It was where she belonged, and damn it, she would fight for it.

Austin sat on the front porch, watching the sun kiss the morning sky.

No sign of Pete. No text. No phone call. The only thing they had was that he'd arrived in Twin City with two other men late last night.

The sound of the front door scraping across the wood caught his attention. "Good morning," he said.

Cinnamon handed him a cup of coffee. "How long have you been awake?"

"Not long," he lied. He'd tossed and turned most of the night. So had Cinnamon, but thankfully, she'd been sound asleep when he'd slipped from the bed at four in the morning.

"You're a terrible liar." She handed him her cell. "Pete texted me an hour ago."

Austin stared at her phone.

Pete: *I'm coming for you and if you know what is best, you will meet me at the ranch entrance at seven a.m. If you're not there, bad things will happen. This is your only warning.*

"I'm glad you didn't respond."

"There's no point." She eased into one of the Adirondack chairs. "Do you think we should change the plan and I should meet him?"

"Are you crazy? Absolutely not. We need to make him come here. He knows this is where you are. He'll come here."

"I don't believe he will," she said. "Not based on that text."

"He wants you back. That's what this is all about."

"That's what I thought too. But maybe he knows that's never going to happen now that I've returned home." She reached out and took Austin's hand. "Before things got really bad, he was so insecure about our relationship. He constantly worried that I would leave him and come running home and that you'd be here to pick up the pieces. I told him that Rosy was his daughter and that I'd never take her away from him. After she died, he did whatever he could to control me. To ensure I wouldn't come to Whiskey Ranch. To you. Now that I have, his worst fear has materialized. He has nothing left to lose."

"That's crazy. He has a lucrative business. He could face real prison time. He has everything to lose, which makes him even more dangerous."

She leaned forward. "When it comes to that part of his life, he's as arrogant as they come. He thinks he's untouchable, like his father. He believes he can buy his way out of trouble. But when it comes to me, he's always thought I was the only woman for him."

"But he cheated on you. That makes no sense."

"It doesn't have to," she said. "Sadly, I know how his brain works. And the more I think about it, the more these two worlds are colliding. If he can't have me, he will make sure you can't either."

"All the more reason for you not to go meet him at the front gate."

"You're not listening to me," she said. "In his wacky mind, if I go to him, it means I've caved. He's won. He can take me and we can go back to our previous life. But if I don't. You won. He lost and that will enrage him. He'll do whatever it takes to take you and this ranch down or end your life and anyone he believes stood in his way."

Austin had to agree she made sense, but he still didn't believe meeting Pete at the gate was the right move. "Brad has two men posing as cowboys right over there." He pointed. "Let me shower, and then I'll call Belmont and see what he says about this text. For now, I want you inside."

"All right. But promise me you'll tell him my thoughts."

"You can be part of the conversation." He leaned in and kissed her cheek. "Come on. You should eat something." Austin tugged at her hand. The next few hours would prove to be the hardest, but after today, he prayed that Pete would be out of their lives.

Cinnamon tossed her backpack over her shoulder and inched toward the main gate. She couldn't believe that Belmont agreed that her plan was the stronger of the two.

Austin had lost his shit, cussing and pacing in the kitchen. He almost didn't let her leave the house. But in the end, this wasn't about what he wanted. It was time to end Pete and his wickedly horrible games.

Quickly, she glanced at her watch.

She was six minutes early. Pete would appreciate that. He hated it when anyone was late. She climbed up on the big boulder outside the gate and waited.

Minutes ticked and not a single car drove by.

It was now five minutes past seven. Her pulse beat in the center of her throat, making it impossible to swallow.

A Range Rover eased to a stop and the passenger side window rolled down.

"Get in," Pete demanded.

"No. Not until you answer a few questions," she managed with a shaky voice.

He laughed. "Not happening."

"I'm going with you, so humor me." She didn't budge from the perch on her rock.

"I have no intention of sitting here arguing with you. Now get in or I'll get out and force you into this car."

"You owe me," she said.

"That's rich. You're the one who has put me in a difficult position with these games." He slipped from the driver's side and stepped around the vehicle's hood, waving a weapon.

Shit. She knew he owned more than one gun and should have known he'd flex his muscles with them, but she hadn't expected he'd do so the second he saw her. "If you want me to go, I want to know what happened to Gage."

"Are you serious right now? Why would I know anything about that man?"

She folded her arms. "Where's Gage? What did you do to him?"

"Nothing." He opened the door. "I'm waiting."

"I want honest answers, and then I will get in and we never have to discuss it again." She sucked in a deep breath. "You do this for me, I'll drop all the charges."

"You're going to do that anyway."

"He was my friend, Pete. He was a kind man who didn't do anything to you." That should push his buttons.

"Not true," Pete said. "He always hated me. He didn't like me dating his daughter. He wouldn't let me take her to prom. Hell, I couldn't even pick her up for a proper date. There wasn't anything *kind* about him."

"Did you hurt him?"

"Gage is fine," Pete said with an exasperated sigh. "The man is as dumb as a doornail. I had one of my men pay him off to disappear for a while."

"Gage wouldn't take your money."

"He would if he thought it would protect you, your cousins, or Austin from harm." He waved his weapon. "Now get in the car."

"How do I know you're telling the truth?"

"Because once you are home and the charges are dropped, I'll tell him he can go back to the ranch. That no harm will come to anyone."

"I want proof now," she said as she jumped from the rock. "Call him and put it on speaker."

"Fine." Pete reached into the car and snagged his cell. He tapped on the screen. It rang twice. "Gage?"

"Yes," Gage's voice flowed through the speaker. It was weak and sad. Not his usual peppy self, but it did sound like him.

"Our arrangement will be coming to an end perhaps next week."

"Cinnamon is okay, yes? Austin is unharmed, yes?" Gage asked.

"Everyone is fine," Pete said. "I'll be in touch." He tossed his phone back inside his SUV. "Satisfied?"

"Actually, no." Something didn't feel right. "Why did you send him away? It doesn't make sense. What difference did it make if he was on the ranch or not?"

"For fuck's sake." Pete lunged forward.

She took three steps back. "I'm serious, Pete. I want answers before I get in your fancy car and go back to our life."

"You can be a real pain in the ass," Pete muttered. "If I couldn't frame Austin for Charity's death, then Gage was my backup."

Cinnamon gasped. "Did you know Charity?"

"Of course I did."

Cinnamon's heart beat faster and faster. "How?"

"Why does it matter?"

"If you want me to go home and be quiet, I want to know all the things I'm shutting my mouth about. I think that's only fair."

"So you can use it against me? No way."

"No," she said. "Knowing will keep me from doing what caused you to bash in my face. This is how we reset and start over. Isn't that what you want?"

"Are you telling me that I've finally gotten through to you?"

"Yes," she said. "Please tell me how you knew Charity."

"I met her while on a trip to Boise. She was in a bar I went to. I couldn't believe it when I found out she was dating Austin. I struck up a friendship. Eventually it became more, but she knew I was married and would never leave my wife."

"You were having an affair with her?"

"Maybe if my wife wasn't so frigid I wouldn't have to." Pete arched a brow. "But I was helping her figure out who she should be with. I encouraged her to pick Austin over Tom. I told her he was the much better catch."

"Did she know you had a history with Whiskey Ranch?"

"Eventually, I told her that I knew of the Whiskey family and that she would learn to love it there if she gave it half a chance. When she called me and told me she was leaving, I tried talking her out of it, but that didn't work."

"So you killed her." Cinnamon narrowed her eyes.

"I took an opportunity to ensure Austin would be out of our lives forever. That man is like a bad rash that won't go away."

"What about Alyssa?" Cinnamon asked before

the police and the FBI could jump out from wherever they were hiding. "Did you kill her and her family too?"

"You are fucking full of questions and I'm so tired of giving you answers. It's time to go home. And I never want you to have contact with anyone on this ranch again."

"You want that, give me this one last thing. I promise, I will never bring up this ranch or my family again. I swear."

"You better not, or you know what will happen," he said. "It was only meant to be a warning. That hadn't been my intention."

"What do you mean a warning?"

"I didn't know they would all get trapped inside. That the house would go up so quickly." He waved his hand. "Let's go."

"Okay." She took one step forward.

Three police cars came flying into the drive.

Pete grabbed her and pressed his weapon against her temple. "You fucking little bitch. You set me up. I'm not going down for this."

Austin appeared fifty feet away, holding a shotgun. He stopped dead in his tracks.

She swallowed. This part she hadn't been prepared for.

Austin lay on his stomach next to his brother-in-law, listening to the woman he loved and Pete. The conversation made him sick to his stomach.

The only saving grace was that Gage was still alive.

As soon as the police cars rolled into the main drive, he jumped to his feet and raced toward Cinnamon.

Only, Pete pressed his weapon to her temple.

If anyone took a shot, if they killed Pete dead, he could still end up shooting Cinnamon.

Austin froze. "Fuck," he mumbled. "What now?"

"We let the FBI talk him down," Brad said. "Let's inch closer, but follow my lead, got it?"

"You're the expert." Austin stayed in line with Brad as they moved closer to the main gates.

"I can't believe you did this to me," Pete's voice came over the comms in Austin's ear. "Now we're both going to die thanks to you."

"It doesn't have to end that way," Belmont said. "Let her go and we can talk demands."

"This is entrapment. It wouldn't stand up in a court of law," Pete said.

Thankfully, even if he didn't confess to Charity's murder, he'd left behind physical evidence that proved he at least was in the vehicle. But they still didn't have the body. That was something that Austin wanted to give her family.

And Tom.

"I don't want Pete to see you," Brad said. "Go to the other—"

"What is that motherfucker doing here?" Pete shifted, staring at Austin. "This is all his fault. We wouldn't even be standing here if it weren't for that asshole."

"Too late," Austin whispered. He sucked in a deep breath, lowering his weapon. No point in antagonizing the asshole any more than he already was.

"I'll kill her," Pete yelled. "Is that what you want, Austin?"

Austin laid his rifle on the ground. He was now twenty feet away. "No. I'd like for you to let her go."

"Not going to happen." Pete held her tight in front of his body. Quickly, he stretched out his arm.

Bang!

Bang!

Cinnamon screamed.

Austin dropped to his knees, gripping his right

thigh. "Fuck. That hurt." His teeth rattled. His muscle felt as though someone had stuffed a grenade inside it and pulled the pin.

"She's next if anyone comes closer," Pete said. "I won't hesitate."

"I've got a clean shot," someone came over the comms system.

"Last chance to put down your weapon," Belmont said.

Pete took a step toward the SUV. "We're getting in the vehicle and driving away. You're not going to follow us, or she's dead. It's that simple."

"If you still have the shot, take it," Belmont whispered.

Bang!

Austin glanced up from his position on the dirt.

Pete fell to the ground. His gun tumbled from his grasp.

Cinnamon took one look at him before taking off running in the direction of Austin.

"I need to stop the bleeding." Brad ripped off his shirt and tied it around Austin's leg. "Did the second shot get you?"

"I don't believe so, but don't you think one is enough," Austin said through gritted teeth.

Brad laughed.

"It's not funny, man." Austin lay back on the hard ground.

"Austin!" Cinnamon stumbled, landing next to him. "Oh my God. Someone call an ambulance."

"Already on the way," Brad said. "He's tough. He'll be fine."

"I'm seeing stars, so I'm not so sure about that." Austin blinked. The sharp pain had turned into an intense throb. "Are you okay?" He took Cinnamon's hand. "Are you hurt?"

"No. I'm fine." She glanced over her shoulder. "I'm not sure I'll be needing a divorce anymore though."

Austin chuckled, but it quickly turned into a cough. "I shouldn't laugh at that."

"I should feel bad, but I kind of don't."

"He murdered people in cold blood," Brad said. "He held you at gunpoint and shot at your boyfriend. I think it's okay to feel relief that this is all behind you."

Sirens rang out in the distance.

Austin stared at the sky. His vision blurred. "This is going to suck."

"What is?" Cinnamon asked.

"Being laid up. Unable to work." He lifted his

head. "I don't think I'll be able to move into the apartment above the bunkhouse."

She bent over and kissed his lips. "You're going to need someone to take care of you for a little while and it's the least I can do, considering you did take a bullet for me, literally."

EPILOGUE

SIX WEEKS LATER...

Austin lay sprawled out on the sofa with the television remote in his hand. He'd flipped through the channels three times and still couldn't find something to hold his attention for more than five minutes. His cell buzzed on the coffee table. He reached for it and groaned. The doctor told him it would be another good three months before he was one hundred percent. The bullet had been lodged in the bone, making the injury more complicated. It required a delicate surgery to remove it and he had to stay in the hospital for two full weeks after.

He wasn't sure what was worse.

The hospital stay or being bedridden at home.

"Hey, Tom." He set his phone on his chest. "How was the service?"

"It was nice. I'm sorry you couldn't be here," Tom said.

"Besides being unable to put weight on this leg, I'm not sure the family would have wanted me there."

"Everyone asked about you," Tom said.

"I'm just glad we could give them—and you—closure." Austin might not have loved Charity, but he never wished her dead. He could only offer her family the ability to find her body and help them lay her to rest. He'd been grateful to the FBI and the local sheriff's department for all their hard work locating where Pete had buried her body.

"How are things with you?" Tom asked.

"I'm healing," he said.

"And Cinnamon?"

A smile spread across Austin's lips. "She's happy to be back with her family. She's all enrolled in college. While she still has nightmares and a shit ton of guilt over things that aren't her fault, she's doing well."

"What about the two of you?"

"For the most part, we're good."

"What is that supposed to mean?" Tom asked.

Since Pete's death, a day hadn't gone by where Austin hadn't spoken to Tom. They had become close friends, which to some seemed odd. However, Austin enjoyed the camaraderie. The more he got to know Tom, the more he realized how much they had in common outside of Charity.

"She has a lot of emotional healing she needs to do and I'm doing my best to give her the space. Sometimes that causes a disagreement."

"That makes no sense."

Austin chuckled. "She thinks I often pull away. But I'm not. I've gone to a couple of her therapy sessions and don't do well." He adjusted his pillows and sat up taller. It was hard for him to discuss this shit with her cousins. It didn't matter that JD was one of his closest friends. Or JW and JB had been in his life since he was a kid. Or he and Irish had been friends forever. They were Cinnamon's cousins and he didn't want to burden them with their problems, which weren't big ones, but still things they needed to work through. "I worry we're rushing things, especially since I need help and she's living here with me. She needed to stand on her own two feet while we discussed how to handle the situation with Pete. However, since I was wounded and he died in the shootout, she's done a bit of a one-eighty."

"She got scared she could have lost you."

"That's what her therapist said, but I'm not going anywhere. I want her to feel like she's in control of her own destiny. To understand she doesn't need me to be whomever she wants. I'm just here to support her."

"You're a good man," Tom said. "I started seeing someone a couple of months ago and I was thinking—when you're feeling up to it—maybe the four of us could get together."

"I'd love that and I'm sure Cinnamon would like it too. But why wait? You should come out to the ranch. I'm going crazy sitting on my ass. I'd love the company."

"Talk it over with Cinnamon and we'll set up a date and time," Tom said. "I still have some of Charity's family here, so I best be going. I just wanted to check in on you."

"Thanks, I appreciate it." Austin ended the call. He tossed his phone to the coffee table, found his crutches, and groaned as he hobbled to the kitchen for a snack. He was supposed to stay off his leg for another two weeks. But he was going nuts doing absolutely nothing but watching television, reading books, and waiting for Cinnamon to return from work.

However, today she embarked on a new chapter in her life.

College.

He was so excited for her and couldn't wait to hear about her first day. She'd always wanted to be a teacher and now she'd get that chance.

The front door swung open.

Shit. He was going to hear hell for being off the sofa. Georgia Moon had come over to feed him lunch and Annette had been by two hours ago to make sure he hadn't needed anything else. Outside of that, he wasn't supposed to do anything.

Two more weeks and he'd be able to put weight on his leg.

But it would still be at least another month before he could return to work.

"What the hell do you think you're doing?" Cinnamon tossed her backpack on the chair by the fireplace and raced to his side.

He eased onto the stool. "I was thirsty." He lifted his big water bottle. "And hungry." He pointed to the bag of popcorn he'd pulled from the cupboard.

"And how did you plan to return that to the sofa?"

"I was going to sit right here," he said like a defiant child.

"You're going to make the healing process longer." She grabbed his drink and the bag. "Do you want help back to the couch?"

"I know how to use these." He waved at the crutches. "They do have me doing things in physical therapy, you know."

She laughed. "I hear you're a big baby."

He rolled his eyes. "How was your day?"

"Amazing. Wonderful. I can't wait to go back tomorrow." She helped him onto the sofa, lifting his bad leg and resting his feet on her lap. "But I feel so old."

"You're far from it."

"Tell that to the eighteen-year-olds who thought I was either the professor or the PA."

He laughed. "I thought you would have been home an hour or so ago. Did you get hit on by all the young studs?"

"That's gross." She shook her head. "I had a doctor's appointment."

He arched a brow. "Therapy? You didn't tell me

you had that today. You know I'm always happy to go."

"No. I went to the gynecologist."

He pounded his chest and coughed. "I guess I didn't need to go to that one."

"Not this time you didn't." She squeezed his foot, rubbing gently. They'd slid into an easy time of living together and he more than enjoyed it. He thrived in their relationship.

Whenever she felt he was too far away emotionally, she told him so and he did his best to adjust. He wanted to please her more than anything, giving her whatever she needed. His biggest concern was never making her feel like he was the one in the driver's seat, which was the dance that had become difficult.

She was used to being in a controlling and manipulative marriage. Pete had stripped her of her ability to make her own decisions. Austin would never be that man, but she often told him that she felt as though he tiptoed around the harder conversations and begged him to stop.

Something that he'd been working on.

"I can't imagine there's any time I'd need to go with you to see that doctor."

"Then you don't understand women or their

bodies as much as I thought you did." She poked his good leg.

"Excuse me?"

"I have an appointment for an ultrasound in a couple of weeks and you will want to be there for that."

"An ultra what? And why? Is something wrong?"

"Are you really that stupid?" She shifted, setting his feet back on the sofa. Straddling his hips, she leaned over and kissed his lips. "Am I hurting you?"

"You asked me that last night when we were in this position and what did I tell you?" He smacked her ass.

"You might have said no, but then you groaned."

He laughed. "That was in throes of pleasure and I'm more than willing to have a repeat of the action. But the bed would be more comfortable."

"I'm sure you are, but what we do in the bedroom is what led me to see the doctor." She pressed her hands on his chest and held his stare. "I can't believe you aren't getting this, so let me recap. I went to see an OB/GYN. That's a doctor who—"

"I know what kind of medicine that doctor practices and there is no reason I would need to go with you…" He let his words trail off. His heart lurched to his throat. His eyes grew wide. "Why do you need an ultrasound? Isn't that something that is used to see babies?"

"Exactly."

"Are you trying to tell me you're pregnant?" His mouth went dry. "I need to sit up."

She moved to the side, helping him to the edge of the sofa. "I haven't gotten my period since returning to Whiskey Ranch."

"And you're just telling me this now?" He tossed his good leg over the side of the couch.

"We've been a little busy between you having surgery and the complications from that surgery. And then there was dealing with the settlement from Pete's death with his family, which came in the mail today, so I can pay you back for my tuition."

"I don't think so." He raked a hand across the top of his head. "If we're going to have a baby together, then whatever is mine is yours." A baby. He couldn't believe it. They had been using condoms, except for that first time.

"For a minute there, I thought you were going to freak out about this."

"Oh, I'm freaking out." He took her hand. "We knew this was a possibility, but when you never brought it up again, I'd sort of put it out of my mind." He kissed her palm. "How are you feeling?"

"Other than I'm a little tired, fine. But I'm more worried about you and whether or not you're happy about this. You're giving me the biggest non-reaction a man who is about to be a dad could possibly give."

"Babe, I've been fantasizing about this moment my entire life. You're the only woman I've wanted to have a family with. I couldn't be more thrilled." He reached for his crutches. "Help me to the bedroom."

"We are not going to go have sex right now."

"Wasn't going to suggest that." He chuckled. "I have something else in mind." He hobbled down the hallway. "I want to give you something."

"What?"

"My mother's engagement ring. It was always supposed to be yours. I know we said we would take things slow, but a baby changes things. Besides, I love you and I always want to be with you."

"Did you just ask me to marry you?"

"It wasn't the best proposal, but that's my intention." He found the ring in the dresser's top drawer and pulled it from the box. He took her hand and placed it on her ring finger.

It was a perfect fit.

"I love you, Cinnamon Cider Whiskey. Will you do me the honor and be my wife?"

"Oh, hell yes." She wrapped her arms around his middle. "But I'm not doing some big-ass wedding. I want a small one right here on the ranch and as soon as possible—before I'm as big as a house."

"Whatever makes you happy." He tossed his crutches to the side and pulled her tight. "I'm going to have to put an addition on this place."

"Oh, I have ideas."

"I'm sure you do," he said. "I need to sit." He plopped his ass on the edge of the bed.

She joined him, resting her head on his shoulder. "We're going to make a wonderful home for our family."

"Our family," he repeated. "You're going to have to keep pinching me, because all of my wildest dreams have come true."

Thank you for taking the time to read Cinnamon Cider Whiskey. Please feel free to leave an honest review.

Also, please check out this series:

Check out _LOVE IN THE ADIRONDACKS!_

Shattered Dreams
An Inconvenient Flame
The Wedding Driver
Clear Blue Sky
Blue Moon
Before the Storm

Grab a glass of vino, kick back, relax, and let the romance roll in…

Sign up for my Newsletter (https://dl.bookfunnel.com/82gm8b9k4y) where I often give away free books before publication.

Join my private Facebook group (https://www.facebook.com/groups/191706547909047/) where I post exclusive excerpts and discuss all things murder and love!

ABOUT THE AUTHOR

Jen Talty is the *USA Today* Bestselling Author of Contemporary Romance, Romantic Suspense, and Paranormal Romance. In the fall of 2020, her short story was selected and featured in a 1001 Dark Nights Anthology.

Regardless of the genre, her goal is to take you on a ride that will leave you floating under the sun with warmth in your heart. She writes stories about broken heroes and heroines who aren't necessarily looking for romance, but in the end, they find the kind of love books are written about :).

She first started writing while carting her kids to one hockey rink after the other, averaging 170 games per year between 3 kids in 2 countries and 5 states. Her first book, IN TWO WEEKS was origi-nally published in 2007. In 2010 she helped form a publishing company (Cool Gus Publishing) with *NY*

Times Bestselling Author Bob Mayer where she ran the technical side of the business through 2016.

Jen is currently enjoying the next phase of her life…the empty nester! She and her husband reside in Jupiter, Florida.

Grab a glass of vino, kick back, relax, and let the romance roll in…

Sign up for my Newsletter (https://dl.bookfunnel.com/82gm8b9k4y) where I often give away free books before publication.

Join my private Facebook group (https://www.facebook.com/groups/191706547909047/) where I post exclusive excerpts and discuss all things murder and love!

Never miss a new release. Follow me on Amazon:amazon.com/author/jentalty

And on Bookbub: bookbub.com/authors/jen-talty

ALSO BY JEN TALTY

Brand new series: SAFE HARBOR!

Mine To Keep

Mine To Save

Mine To Protect

Mine to Hold

Mine to Love

Check out LOVE IN THE ADIRONDACKS!

Shattered Dreams

An Inconvenient Flame

The Wedding Driver

Clear Blue Sky

Blue Moon

Before the Storm

NY STATE TROOPER SERIES (also set in the Adirondacks!)

In Two Weeks

Dark Water

Deadly Secrets

Murder in Paradise Bay

To Protect His own

Deadly Seduction

When A Stranger Calls

His Deadly Past

The Corkscrew Killer

First Responders: A spin-off from the NY State Troopers series

Playing With Fire

Private Conversation

The Right Groom

After The Fire

Caught In The Flames

Chasing The Fire

Legacy Series

Dark Legacy

Legacy of Lies

Secret Legacy

Emerald City

Investigate Away

Sail Away

A Little Bit Whiskey

It's all in the Whiskey

Johnnie Walker

Georgia Moon

Jack Daniels

Jim Beam

Whiskey Sour

Whiskey Cobbler

Whiskey Smash

Irish Whiskey

The Monroes

Color Me Yours

Color Me Smart

Color Me Free

Color Me Lucky

Color Me Ice

Color Me Home

Search and Rescue

Protecting Ainsley

Protecting Clover

Protecting Olympia

Protecting Freedom

Protecting Princess

Protecting Marlowe

Fallport Rescue Operations

Searching for Madison

Searching for Haven

Searching for Pandora

Searching for Stormi

DELTA FORCE-NEXT GENERATION

Shielding Jolene

Shielding Aalyiah

Shielding Laine

Shielding Talullah

Shielding Maribel

Shielding Daisy

The Men of Thief Lake

Rekindled

Destiny's Dream

Federal Investigators

Jane Doe's Return

The Butterfly Murders

THE AEGIS NETWORK

The Sarich Brother

The Lighthouse

Her Last Hope

The Last Flight

The Return Home

The Matriarch

Aegis Network: Jacksonville Division

A SEAL's Honor

Talon's Honor

Arthur's Honor

Rex's Honor

Kent's Honor

Buddy's Honor

Aegis Network Short Stories

Max & Milian

A Christmas Miracle

Spinning Wheels

Holiday's Vacation

The Brotherhood Protectors

Out of the Wild

Rough Justice

Rough Around The Edges

Rough Ride

Rough Edge

Rough Beauty

The Brotherhood Protectors

The Saving Series

Saving Love

Saving Magnolia

Saving Leather

Hot Hunks

Cove's Blind Date Blows Up

My Everyday Hero – Ledger

Tempting Tavor

Malachi's Mystic Assignment

Needing Neor

Holiday Romances

A Christmas Getaway

Alaskan Christmas

Whispers

Christmas In The Sand

Heroes & Heroines on the Field

Taking A Risk

Tee Time

A New Dawn

The Blind Date

Spring Fling

Summers Gone

Winter Wedding

The Awakening

Fated Moons

The Collective Order

The Lost Sister

The Lost Soldier

The Lost Soul

The Lost Connection

The New Order